PRAISE FOR EMERGENCY PLAN -OR- DOOMSDAY LIST (DANI SERIES BOOK ONE)

"...The prose is sharp, conversational, and unapologetically direct, giving the book the feel of a personal confession crossed with a challenge issued straight to the reader. While the tone may alienate those looking for a gentler motivational arc, it will resonate strongly with readers who appreciate honesty without cushioning..."

— MEGAN, VERIFIED PURCHASER

"...The writing style is sharp, conversational, and deliberately uncomfortable. It reads like a mix of confession and direct challenge, making the reader feel as though they are being addressed personally. This tough-love approach is the book's strongest quality, as it makes Dani's growth feel realistic and earned. However, the blunt tone may come across as heavy-handed for readers who prefer a softer or more nuanced exploration of personal struggles...."

— JOHN, VERIFIED PURCHASER

"...The book emphasizes that life does not guarantee equal opportunities, but it does deliver consequences. Through Dani's struggles, the narrative highlights the dangers of waiting passively for change. It insists that while setbacks are inevitable, individuals are not required to remain trapped by them. The message is clear: survival and progress demand effort, honesty, and resilience...."

— CAROLINE, VERIFIED PURCHASER

DANI SERIES
BOOK ONE

EMERGENCY PLAN
- Or -
DOOMSDAY LIST

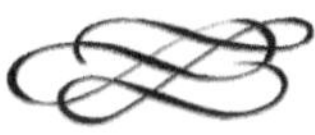

ALSO BY H. R. NOVELTON

A Message To Tiger Lily

DANI SERIES
BOOK ONE

EMERGENCY PLAN
- Or -
DOOMSDAY LIST

H.R. NOVELTON

&

DANI SENTINI

H.R. NOVELTON, LLC

A story my father told me once:
The neighbor walked over from his house
and said to the man painting his own
house on a ladder, "Why do we do it?
What's it all about?" The painter looked
down at him and said,"When you boil it
all down, all we really have is our children."
—Dani Sentini

"They can say an awful lot of things,
Marian, but nobody can say you were wrong."
—Dani Sentini

PREFACE

All characters are fictional. Any character resembling a real person is purely coincidental. Except where obvious, names of businesses are fictional, and any resemblance to a real operating business is coincidental.

Nothing herein is intended to offer dietary, healthcare, or financial advice. Before starting any diet, you should consult with your doctor. If you are struggling with weight and self-image issues, you should consult with a healthcare professional to determine what your ideal weight should be, and you should not lose more weight than is recommended by your doctor.

The fictional characters featured in this book, including its author Dani Sentini, are merely expressing their opinions and ideas. However, books and authors referenced herein are real, although the author of this book has no financial interest in the sale of their books or products.

This is not a diet book. Not all of Marian's dietary opinions are consistent with the conclusions of doctors and professional dietitians. Marian herself admits she is not basing her dietary assertions solely on the advice of a nutritionist; many of her suggestions come from commonly known diets that can be found on the internet. It is true that everyone should take the time to research foods and dietary supplements and make their own dieting plan; for this, we recommend you consult with a healthcare or dietary professional.

Before taking any dietary supplements or using alternative therapies and curative products, you should always ask the advice of your healthcare professional. Self-treating for any medical condition should be done under the guidance of your healthcare professional and with due diligence on your part. Self-treating without the advice of your healthcare professional is very risky. Marian's assertions are based on her own opinions. A product or practice that may work for one individual may not work for another. What you do to eliminate the symptoms of a disease does not necessarily mean you have cured the disease. We support a holistic approach to healthcare.

The one thing on which all healthcare professionals agree is the importance of a healthy diet and age-appropriate exercise.

The purpose of this work is for entertainment and to generally remind readers of the importance of 1) improving one's health through improving one's diet and lifestyle habits and by remembering the interconnectedness of taking care of your body and mind and pursuing your short- and long-term goals; and 2) improving one's financial well-being by using commonly known principles that are proven successful. Success normally requires working hard, making personal sacrifices, and living a disciplined lifestyle.

Any financial advice offered by Marian or anyone else in this story is based on their own experiences and opinions. The main point of this aspect of my story is to assert my belief that independent wealth is achievable for anyone who is able and willing to work. It helps a great deal to develop your talents and success skills, a major component of which is your willingness to work hard, have a positive outlook, and to smile frequently. Like freedom itself, success in any endeavor does not come without discipline, sacrifice, and hard work, nor is it guaranteed. One thing is certain: if you don't believe success is possible, then for you it probably won't be.

On the other hand, Marian, our red-caped advisor, says one does not need to be rich to be independently wealthy, nor do they need to be independently wealthy to be successful and happy. Independent financial security can be achieved by anyone able and willing to work, and Marian explains how there are many roads that lead there, but none of them go by way of self-defeatism, blaming others for your miseries and hardships, resenting those who are already successful, laziness in caring for yourself and the spaces around you, and expecting others to provide for you.

In my view, any politician who supports the welfare state and whose policies invoke terms like Social Justice, Equity, or Climate Justice, are poverty pimps and should be voted out of office, as their ideology is based in Marxism, which aligns itself with mediocrity and subjugation. Marxism is antithetical to individual freedom and the pursuit of individual goals and aspirations; and it certainly does not place anyone on the road to earning those rewards which should follow individual achievement. The American Dream is real and it is achievable in most countries, although we acknowledge that it suffers from ill health because governments everywhere are gradually falling under the control of Marxist mobs which are working hard and doing their utmost to kill it. That includes many sectors of the American government.

Harmony Mountain is a fictional place. While scientists are discovering the powerful therapeutic effects of crystals, light, and resonant sound waves, the story about Harmony Mountain's Healing Cavern is fictional. But it is not fiction that a good walk up a mountain can be very therapeutic and healthy.

Nor is it fictional, in my opinion, that if ever they did discover the fountain of youth, or a real "healing cavern," our government would do all in its power to conceal it, fence it off from the rest of us, and turn it into a spa for the rich and famous.

All that I've said above notwithstanding, every word of Marian's advice and recommendations has worked just splendidly for me.

— Dani Sentini

1

The woman in the red cape is walking against the sharp February breeze, wearing a red-hooded cape and black gloves, and carrying a brown paper bag. She's holding the bag like you might carry a baby to keep it warm. Dani Sentini has seen her many times before. She's always on the opposite side of the street and in all sorts of weather. It's like she's unfazed. And it's in the afternoon always, like she's coming home from work and has stopped off at Fletcher's Market to pick up some things. She comes from the left and moves to the right down Morgan Street, and Dani stands up from her desk, leans over, and watches her go by. The woman keeps going till she goes down behind a row of old maple trees. Who could she be, wearing that red cape like that? It's like she fell from the sky from an old fairy tale. All she needs is a wolf walking beside her with a big fat smile on his face.

Dani returns to her seat at her desk—an old wooden office desk with an old wooden chair. Both came from a garage sale. The desk is scratched, and you need a blotter or the writing will show the scratches through the paper. A student scratched their name in the corner—Reggie. Chances are good Reggie is dead now. But the chair is a fancy swivel type, but also made of oak, a pedestal chair so old it has only four lateral legs on squeaky steel casters—probably came out of the nineteenth century and perhaps the first swivel chair ever made. Maybe its maker's name was Swivel—an old guy smoking a pipe. But Dani wanted it the moment she saw it. An old wood chair like that has character with its curving backrest made with square spindles, the curved arms and the solid feel of it. A writer sitting in a chair like that, soaking up all its ancient memories…well, she would simply be a better writer. And for twenty dollars how could one pass it up?

But the man warned her to watch out. "There are only four legs. You could tip over."

He had looked at her and said it and she knew where he was looking—a girl with such fat hips, a top-heavy girl.

Watch out, you could tip over!

While listening to one of Enya's CDs, which causes her to feel both peaceful and expansive, she's been doing her homework, a math assignment. The ninth graders are learning about household economics this semester. On this topic, she is focused on the increase in prices of groceries from year to year when the prices keep rising. This is not an easy topic to understand, even though the book explains it in clear illustrations.

For example, there's an illustration of a jar of honey which weighs sixteen ounces and costs five dollars. A year later, the jar costs five dollars and twenty cents, but is now only twelve ounces. The problem is a simple word problem requiring a yes or no answer:

If Donald's wife, William, made five hundred dollars per week last year and this year she makes five hundred and twenty dollars, is her income keeping up with the increase in the actual cost of the honey that her husband, Donald, has to pay?

[ ] Yes [ ] No.

The perplexing problem gives Dani a headache despite Enya. In the first place, why did they reduce the size to twelve ounces? Secondly, figuring out all these percentages isn't going to help you cough up the extra twenty cents to pay for less honey than you got before. Donald'll just have to decide if he wants to buy it, and if he does buy it, maybe William can figure a way to use less. Maybe she can mix a little water with it like Mom does with other things, like milk, prune juice, and frozen orange juice concentrate, and hope that her husband, Donald, doesn't notice.

Dani is allowed to use a calculator to complete her math assignments. Her teacher even lets her use the calculator for the quizzes and exams. In fact, she's even allowed to use her textbook during exams. But this seems not to be much help as her math grades hover somewhere around B with an occasional C thrown in for good measure.

You're not trying, Dani!

It's like a lot of her other classes. Her absolute worst grades are in gym class where she gets constant C minuses to D minuses, and several times she's gotten F's for not completing a unit. Units! These are like track, softball, basketball, tennis, trampoline, gymnastics. You get the idea. There's even a unit for relay races. God help us! And you're probably smart enough to figure out which ones she fails to complete. Well, if you guessed trampoline and gymnastics, you'd be about right. As for the others, Dani sees mostly C minuses and D's, and to be honest, those grades are generous.

But you have to think about this. The trampoline? Seriously? For her, climbing on a trampoline would be about the same as walking on a tightrope at a circus—without a net! And the gymnastic equipment? There's another one. Is there anybody who actually thinks she could swing for more than two seconds on the rings? Or on the parallel bars? If she tries to hurdle the horse, somebody will get a video of it and put it on the internet, where it'll go viral. Whatever she manages to do on this equipment, she looks like a big fat bounding ball of Jell-O. No thanks!

Oh, then there's the rope. What a laugh that is! No matter how hard she tries, she can't climb up the rope to higher than six inches off the floor, which is accomplished not by climbing, but by jumping. The higher she jumps, the higher she can climb. The measurement is augmented substantially if she holds her feet up and curls her toes.

Nor can she do one whole and complete pushup without a little help from placing her knees on the floor. Nor can she conquer even the first inch of one whole and complete chin-up. For chin-ups, it seems standard for most of the class to get a toe-hold on the wall and leverage up. Then there's the God-blessed laps around the track. This is achieved by making tiny little steps. It's a trick she learned from several of the other girls whose gym grades are as bad or worse than hers. A bit of solace in that.

But then there's English. Dani excels at English. That is, she excels in writing. Although, to be honest, her grades rarely go above a B, as she doesn't follow too many of the rules of grammar. Her teacher, Mrs. Leaf, is a freaking stickler, scoring her down for the tiniest irregularities.

But Dani complains: "I write free style. It's my own voice. Language is changing, you know. I do know the rules."

Then she makes up words. Like for example the word for when you have a good and balanced perspective of things—circumspective. Right there is a great word that should be in the dictionary, but it isn't.

"There's no such word, Dani."

"Well, clearly, there ought to be."

Thank goodness her writing skills are greatly influenced by her talent for writing stories on topics Mrs. Leaf likes to read about and to say things she likes to hear; otherwise, her grade would hover around a C+. For example, her essay on why boys should be allowed to compete in girls' sports if they identify as girls; and why girls should be allowed to play boys' sports if they identify as boys. It's a simple matter of mind over matter. If a girl thinks she's a boy, she's a boy. If a boy thinks he's a girl, so be it—she's a he and he's a she. And they should also go to the locker room of their chosen gender. If the mind is the most powerful organ, a child should have a right to decide certain things for themselves.

Following this logic, Dani's *thoughtful essay* (Mrs. Leaf's term) went on circumspectively to assert that students should also grade their own papers and give themselves the score they feel they've earned. Therefore, they should be allowed to move to any grade level at will—depending on their having good grades. Most importantly, they should assign onto themselves their own chosen age group. Unfortunately, Mrs. Leaf gave her an A for the paper, not because she recognized it for the spoof that it was, but because she was at least tepidly inclined to agree.

But Dani, God help her, has a new essay to write now. This one for Home Economics class—Mrs. Kanbury: *prepare a grocery list, go to a grocery store and buy some groceries for your home, prepare a meal for your family, and, in a minimum of five typed and double-spaced pages, write about your experience.* It's like a term paper due at the end of the semester, and it's already nearly March! And, reading the assignment again to be sure, it has to be at least five full typed and double-spaced pages long! It was assigned in January, and she's been putting it off.

FIVE FULL PAGES?!

2

A knock on her bedroom door draws her attention to the clock on the wall.

"Dani!"

It's her older brother, Crazy Louie.

"It's time to start dinner! I'm starving!"

"Start it yourself. I'm doing homework."

Crazy Louie bangs on the door. "Come *on!* I'm starving to death! Right *now!*"

BANG! BANG! BANG!

"You're not my boss!" she shouts.

"I am so your boss!" He tries the door knob, but it's locked. "Come *on!*"

"It's spaghetti and meatballs! You can boil water, can't you?!"

"I don't know how to make spaghetti *or* meatballs!"

"The meatballs are frozen. All you do is put em in a pan and heat them. Can you follow the instructions on the spaghetti box? Oh, I'm sorry. I forgot you can't read!"

"Shut up! You're supposed to make dinner. I shovel the driveway."

"I shoveled it last time and the walk, too."

"I was at Dad's."

"Anyway, it hardly ever snows."

"I take out the garbage and mow the lawn and rake the leaves."

"Why is the grass always tall? The porch has garbage all over the place. And why do I see leaves everywhere?"

"You're an idiot, you know it? A total idiot!"

His complaints are pathetic. Dani shuts off her iPhone, where she's been texting her friend, Cindy Rand, on the topic of Jason Ash, whose name is Ashbakker, but no one ever calls him that. He's the cutest boy in the school, he's on the football and basketball teams, and Cindy's been dating him and having sex with him, and it's all she can talk about and all Dani wants to hear about. How could she ever fathom the mysteries of boys and sex if she didn't have a friend like Cindy?

Dani gets up and goes out there. She pushes her seventeen-year-old brother aside and goes down to the kitchen where she starts dinner, only to find there are only five meatballs in the bag and half a jar of tomato sauce. She compensates for the lack of sauce by adding water; and for the lack of meatballs by adding pasta—another clever trick of her mother's. There's also a small chunk of Romano cheese left over from a week ago. She grates this into the sauce to thicken it. There's one tomato left in the crisper and she takes and slices this and throws it into the pasta pan, too. Amazingly, she then finds a hamburger left over from some past meal. She sniffs under the lid. It doesn't seem to stink. She cuts it into small pieces and in it goes. Again, her mother knows many tricks of the trade and this is a good way to get rid of an old left-behind hamburger. To enhance the flavor she adds some oregano, garlic, and red pepper. Although Crazy Louie hates garlic, he'll like the extra red pepper. It'll provide a more robust flavor to compensate for the thin sauce, kind of like *thickening the extender* —words Dani's picked up from Mrs. Kanbury who happens to be a big fan of thrift.

"It's ready!"

Crazy Louie comes lumbering down from his room. He piles his plate full, taking three of the five meatballs and most of the hamburger pieces. He gets a can of diet cola and grabs a small bag of onion-flavored potato chips, taking these into his diet cola hand.

"Thanks for offering to split the meatball!" she calls as he goes out, making a face at him behind his back. He goes up and slams his bedroom door.

Dani takes the rest of the spaghetti, the two meatballs and burger pieces, what sauce is left, and with her own diet cola and her own bag of chips goes to her room, locking the door behind her.

3

Dani's mother comes home from work at eleven-thirty. You would never know she's an emergency room nurse because she disposes of all her uniforms before leaving the hospital. She doesn't eat evening meals at home because she can eat for free at the hospital cafeteria. It's one of the perks of being a high-ranking nurse, virtually on call twenty-four/seven. For this reason, Dani has given a lot of thought to becoming a nurse so she can eat all she wants for free, too.

But her mom does have a nighttime snack, usually in the form of a lite beer; and certainly she'll have a beer if she's had a rough night. For Mom, a rough night would be if she has to deal with some kid's broken arm from skateboarding in the park or a skier's broken leg. Certainly anything involving blood and pain-causing injuries. That's because Crazy Louie and Dani both ski.

Skiing for Dani requires a tenuous set of snowplowing and side-to-side skidding skills. To stop, you have to plan your moves so as to skid and turn a little up the hill, or at least across it. After you've stopped and are fully under control again, then you turn and take a new tack across the slope, skidding more and easing to a stop again. This way avoids going faster than one can run, which is plenty fast enough. It takes a bit of time getting down the hill, but you get there in one piece.

One thing it certainly does not do is keep up with Cindy Rand. Cindy can get down and back up the hill by the time Dani gets halfway down. But she avoids cracking her head on a tree and mostly it avoids going ka-plop.

So it isn't Dani that causes her mother to worry. It's Crazy Louie. Crazy Louie is one big fat accident waiting to happen. *Hazard* should have been his middle name. He's probably the most likely kid in town to break an arm or leg, or his entire head, skateboarding at Stacy Ann Hastings Memorial Park on any given day of the year. Snowboarding on the nearby slopes puts him at high risk of paying his mother a visit in the ER.

But, of course, any injured or sick kid can stress Mom badly enough to require a beer when she gets home from her shift.

"What happened tonight?" Dani asks her upon entering the kitchen.

"A little girl about seven had an ear infection. Really very bad. She should have seen a doctor days ago and gotten amoxicillin for it. But they wait till it gets very bad, then bring them to the emergency room where it costs five times as much. But that doesn't matter when you don't have to pay for it."

"How do they not have to pay for it?"

"Medicare pays for it."

"How come it doesn't pay for Dad?"

"Because we have insurance and he's covered by it."

"Why don't you take him off your insurance?"

"We're still married. I can't take him off."

"So why won't insurance pay for his operation?"

"Because he's on insurance that requires approval first and there's been no doctor that recommends it. Too risky. No assurance of benefit. Efficacy. Risk of further injury. They usually don't approve those."

"Why isn't he looking around for somebody to approve it?"

"Even if somebody approved it, he's still gotta pay the deductible plus all the out-of-pocket co-insurance. That comes to a lot of money when you're not working, especially after you're already paying for the expensive premium, which I'm paying half of, but he's still gotta dish out a lotta money for it. And why don't you ask me to divorce him? That right there's a solution."

"Cause I don't want you to divorce him. I want you to get with it and win him back. I bet he's got his fill of old Margie Fuller by now."

"Aren't you so sweet and silly! What he's got is his fill of pain meds and sleeping pills!"

Her mother sips her beer there and tells about another case of somebody breaking their ankle at the skating rink. "I'll tell you, it's one thing or another," she says. "I'm sure glad you kids don't ice skate—all the broken wrists and ankles I see! And heads, too! They ought to wear helmets!" Otherwise, her mother doesn't say much.

Although the house isn't even close to being neat, her mother never complains unless the dishes aren't all washed and put away. She asks about Dani's day, and Dani tells her about the insane homework and its stupid question about the honey.

"The answer's no," she says.

"It is? How do you, like, know that so easy?"

"Cause William's pay has increased the same percentage as the jar of honey has. The only difference is the jar is smaller. So no, William's salary hasn't kept up with the cost of the honey."

"Huh."

"And by the way," she says, "That thing they do with the size of containers? Making everything smaller? That's a neat little trick. They do that all the time, making packages smaller and hoping we won't notice, cause we're just a bunch of blind mice. Tunafish is a good one. Coffee. Even spaghetti and sauce. It's all getting to be less and less, and the prices still go up!"

Her mother sips her beer and asks, "And what's all this with Donald and William anyway? What's that all about?"

"You don't wanna know, Mom. Believe me, you just don't wanna freaking know."

"Good, then I won't ask."

"But I do have a question on that," says Dani.

"What's that?"

"Well, okay, with Donald and William—so you have two guys who are married, right?"

"Alright. So they're gay. Big deal."

"No, no, wait," says Dani. "So William identifies as a woman, right? Cause he's the wife. And Donald, he's the husband. So if they're husband and wife, and identify as male and female, then technically they're not gay." Dani looks at her with big eyes, waiting for an answer.

"Seriously! You're asking me this!"

Laughing: "Yes. Are they gay or straight?"

Her mother rolls her eyes. "You know, if I had the money, I'd take you out of that school and put you in a private school. I oughta complain. That's what I oughta do! I oughta write a damned letter!"

"Please don't. I have all I can handle without my mother becoming a crusader."

"God help you poor children! It's no wonder Crazy Louie's crazy. How is it that *you're* not?"

"Don't worry, I'm getting there."

"That boy, I tell you. Every night I go in to work and I think this'll be the night, this'll be the night. An ambulance pulls up and the doors open and I'm thinking, *oh my god, here he comes. What's he broken now?*"

"They never brought him in an ambulance, Mom. You or Dad brought him or he took himself."

"Your dad brought him with the broken nose he got at Sky Peak."

"When he did a face plant in the halfpipe doing a backflip," adds Dani. "And you brought him when he broke his elbow at the skate park."

"And he brought himself when he broke his arm on the BMX halfpike," says her mom.

"Halfpipe," says Dani.

"What?"

"It's called a halfpipe."

"Whatever."

"And he brought himself the time he broke his arm," says Dani.

"Ha, ha, yes. He come in with his broken arm, and somebody comes in and gets me and I gotta go out there and check him in and then I gotta give him his X-ray. God help me! And all the other nurses are all around, and it's like he's dying or something, and then they come and say, *isn't he brave? Most boys that age would be crying. But he's laughing and making jokes, saying for them to hurry up so he can get back to the park.* And I'm saying, like *Hey, he's serious! If you let him out of here, he will! He'll hop on that dirty little bike of his and go back to the damned park!"*

Her mom sips her beer and adds, "Well, they don't call him Crazy Louie for nothing! He fears nothing! When dogs chase him, he turns around and chases them! And now they're always asking me how's your son? How's Louie? And I say *he's just as crazy as he ever was! He'll probably be in to see us tonight!"*

Conni, her mother, goes upstairs and checks in with him, and if there's anything Mr. Crazy can possibly complain about, he complains about it in a complaining monotone that reverberates through the walls, doors, and floors. Dani takes up her mom's beer and sips a little and listens. On this night, she can hear his voice going on and on about something, and she can pretty well guess what it is, after hearing her own name droning through the floor. But her mother comes back downstairs and says nothing, and Dani, feeling relief that her mom's home, now feels a wave of sleepiness and says good night, feeling a little calmer from the beer also.

But a thought comes to her, and she stops and turns.

4

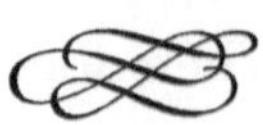

ani stops and turns and says, "Mom, we're out of a lot of stuff. Can I go to the store tomorrow after school?"

"What are you out of already?"

"Oh, come on!" Dani lists things she knows of.

"Alright." Her mother goes to her purse and takes out her wallet, then takes out a twenty.

"Mom, I'm not going to the movies!"

Pursing her lips, her mother takes out another twenty.

"That's still not enough."

"You two don't exactly look like you're starving, you know."

"Neither do you."

"You better watch yourself! Taking a tone!" She takes out another twenty. "Here then. Get enough for the week. I'm taking a long shift over the weekend. I'm not going to be around much."

"Thank you."

"Well, thank you for doing it. Sorry I haven't been around much."

"You know, it's very strange that you have two jobs and Dad doesn't even have one," says Dani.

"He's still managing his business. He'll be better soon."

Dani scoffs. "He's not managing anything. He's got Margie and Landers the foreman. He's hardly involved at all. And Margie says Landers isn't exactly top brass. That whole business is sliding downhill. She tells me what's going on alright."

Her mother looks up sharply. "He's doing the best he can."

"You keep saying that but you know it isn't true. I've talked to him, Mom. I know that if he gets back on the job, he loses his disability. He's not going back to work!"

Her mother pauses and stares at her with a look of frustration. "Alright. So you have a little taste of the insanity that's out in the world. I guess your school has prepared you for it—one thing they do right. So—fine—there you have it. Your dad's not going back to work, nor is he even allowed to mow his own lawn, even if he could. They spy on people with disabilities to make sure they're really disabled." Her mother pauses and adds, "Anyway, your dad's been in pain since his injury and now he's addicted to his drugs and can't get off them, even if he *could* get better."

Her mom takes another long sip of the beer.

"Is this the reason you've taken up with the beer lately?"

"You just never mind about me having a beer now and then!"

"Alright, but what's that mean—if he *could* get better?"

"I mean if his injury went away tomorrow, he'd still be addicted to his pain meds, a fact which would still render him effectively disabled. He's on disability, he's addicted to drugs, the pins in his back are junk, and I doubt he'll ever be able to work again. He can't even go out to the porch to pick up the damned newspaper!"

"So you're saying he's totally finished? He's never going back to building houses? He's never working again at all, forever?"

Her mother stares at her, a bit exasperated. "Honey, half the time he needs help just going to the bathroom. No. He's not going back to work."

"Then why have you been talking all this time about his getting back into the business?"

"You're giving me a headache now. It's like everything else in the world today. There's nothing but chaos. We try to think and be rational and logical and hopeful, but the world has lost any hope of logic or rational thought. You know, like maybe it might be better in the long run to have left the broken disk in and let it heal, even if that means being in a cast for a year. But no, no. We've invented a way for doctors and hospitals to earn an extra fifty thousand by removing the disk and installing hardware. What could go wrong with that? Huh? *Oh, gee, we're sorry! We forgot to tighten the screws! But we can't fix it cause now there's a bunch of other problems and we can't fix those either, and how come he went back to work and started lifting the ladders all over again that caused the problem in the first place? Well, that's because you f——in' told him he could!*

Her mom sits there with her beer and looks away, maybe thinking of going on with more, but then deciding not to.

"The system is broken, my dear child," she says finally. "You'll have to get adjusted to it. But not me! I won't! I guess I'm too old to adjust. I guess I'm just stuck in a time warp!" Her mother's eyes look so sad and are maybe starting to tear up.

Dani takes up the beer and finishes it. She crinkles the can and tosses it and gets her mom another, and Conni takes it.

"How much does he make from disability?" asks Dani.

"Enough to pay his bills, not much else. He's behind on his credit card. Maxed out one and gone on to another. Do you know he's been paying for business expenses with his credit cards?!"

There's another pause, and Conni takes a sip of the new beer and wipes her eyes while Dani thinks.

"So, if you're counting on him paying for your Ski Club and buying you all sorts of new clothes like he did before, you better adjust your expectations. His back is not getting better. There is no healing of anything. He's getting worse by the day, along with his business. And I'm no better off cause I'm trying to help him out. The fool that I am! He goes off with another woman and leaves us high and dry, and I'm sending them money! Me! I must be the biggest idiot God ever put on this earth!"

"He didn't leave us."

Her mother, Conni Sentini, looks up sharply from the beer and Dani takes it up again and takes a swig and says, "You left."

Her mother bristles at this narrative, which is true but doesn't correspond with her preferred storyline.

"How'd we get *here*, Mom? How'd we end up in this apartment?"

"What do you think I should have done? Should I have just looked the other way? Ignored his little Margie Fuller and gone on like nothing was going on?"

"I don't know."

"What would you have done?"

"I don't know. I'm just saying it wasn't Dad that decided who lives where. It was you. I don't like it when you say it was him. Your version of things got me to hating him. Cause *you* hated him!"

"You just wait," says her mom. "You just wait and see how you'll feel when it happens to you. You'll see."

Her mom starts to really sniffle now, wiping her eyes with a napkin there.

"I'm not judging you, Mom. I might have done the same thing. But for now, we need to make some changes cause this just isn't working out. There's gotta be a better way to manage this house."

"If you saw our bills and rent compared to what I make. . .and how much I've been giving to your dad for all his bills, you'd wonder why *we're* not standing out in front of Corina's Diner with tin cups and shopping carts."

Dani eyes the sixty dollars in her hand. She looks down at her mother there, as a wave of sadness sweeps through her.

5

Growing up had been a happy time—a time split between here in Languishire and Silverdale fifty miles away. Silverdale's where she and Crazy Louie, before he was called that, used to spend most of their summers with Grandma and Grandpa Sentini on their dairy farm at the foot of Harmony Mountain. How exciting it had been when school let out and they'd go home and pack their clothes in brown paper bags and Mom would put them on the bus or Dad would drive them to the farm— his old home. And how exciting it was to drive there on Route 30 staring straight ahead to see all the grays and greens rising larger as their car seemed to go right up into the sky. Dad liked to talk about the times he had there—the mountain and the farm—and he talked a lot about his old friend Young Indian Joe. He and Young Indian Joe, he used to say, *knew the mountain like the back of our hands.*

And many times her best friend Cindy would come with her. It was like going to another planet, just the two of them, mostly hiking up and down the trails to the different peaks, the springs and especially to Healing Cavern and its warm bath. There was also the swimming in Lake Clear and Prism Lake. And how she and Cindy and Crazy Louie used to help her grandparents with the farm work. But it wasn't work. It was all fun.

Now and then during the heavy time of haying, her father would come and stay over a few days at a time to help. It was always better when he was there because he'd take her and Cindy and sometimes Louie to Nigh Peak and they'd have lunch and fly kites all afternoon. They always got the kites at a little store in Montclear and it seemed her father was like a little boy whenever he went into that store. They sold every kind of thing that flew in the wind, but he preferred the regular old diamond kites and bought the red ones like his father Luigi always had. Sometimes Luigi came with them and other times it was just Cindy and her there. Eventually the farm ceased operating and the land was leased to the neighbor.

Anymore, it's hard to think of her father, Angie, as having been a farmer, a mountain hiker, or a kite flyer. It was hard to imagine herself as the daughter of farmers. Not only that, but she's the granddaughter of a member of the Northeast Tribes—an Indian. No, seriously, a real in-the-blood tribes girl. But that was long ago on a planet far, far away.

And having gotten fat hasn't exactly kept her feeling connected to that otherworldly life, has it? Exactly when was the last time she did more than stick her feet in a mountain lake? But there really had been those times. There had been the old days. There had been the cows and riding on tractors and making forts in the haymow where she and Cindy played. Yes, there had been Cindy and Craggy Ledge and the million-dollar vistas and all those dreams they shared. Seems at that time there had been real happiness and a real future full of promise.

When it's in theory, everything's simple.

"That'll get us through a few days," says her mother, patting her hand there. "See if you can stretch it."

Dani holds up the three twenties there and says scoffingly, "All the hours you and all those nurses put in at the hospital! . . . and what they pay you!"

"You're telling me? Here, let me get you some paper and a pen and you can write a letter. Send it to the newspaper. I'm sure they'll read it and we'll all get a big fat pay raise!" Her mother leans back in the chair laughing, but makes no move to actually get the paper and pen, only lifting the beer up for another sip.

Dani doesn't quite see the humor and stares at her, saying, "You're sure in a mood today!"

"Please, it's a fact of life, honey. You're never going to be paid what you're worth. That's in the system, too. If you're not handing over your money to a damned landlord, you'll be handing it to a damned bank, and that's after the damned government gets done taking their damned taxes out of you. Take our phone bill, twenty to thirty percent of it is taxes and fees! This beer? About forty percent is taxes! A lot of people are borrowing money just to put food on the table or a shirt on their back. It's why I won't use a credit card. That's another system that's messed up badly. Look at all the trouble that's caused us. Your dad pays a hundred dollars on his credit bill? Most of it goes to pay the interest."

"What's *interest?*"

"Seriously? Don't they teach you *anything* at that school except about Donald and William?"

"We haven't got to interest yet. We're still on inflation. But, yes, that'll be another Donald and William story. They're on just about every page, except for when it's Nancy and Samantha."

"Well, interest and inflation are just two ends of the same candle. You'll find that out soon enough."

Dani remembers the idea she's been kicking around and says, "Mom, since I do most of the cooking around here, why don't you let me get all the groceries from now on? I'll keep track of what we use and what we need, and then we won't be running out of things. We hardly had any meatballs and sauce tonight. I could work up a budget. Planning ahead, I'm sure I could save a lot of money."

"Alright. You might as well jump right in. The sooner you learn, the better off you'll be, and I won't have all the complaints. You show me you've got what it takes to be frugal and smart, and I'll turn the whole bank account over to you and let you handle our money, what little there is of it. I sure can't say I'm any good at it."

"Didn't they teach economics when you were in high school?" Dani asks.

"Home Ec? I think they covered the home part pretty well, but I don't remember they taught much about economics that was ever useful."

6

$\mathcal{D}$ani goes up to her room thinking about her new big responsibility—the official House Cook, Meal Planner, and maybe its Money Manager. A kind of boss. If she's good at it, maybe she can even help her father get through his rough times. After she undresses for bed, she passes by the tall mirror on her door and looks into it, standing there and taking her time to take in the image of her body. Her mother was not exaggerating. If a stranger saw this body, he'd surely agree: she doesn't look undernourished, and by the look of her fat legs, bulging and over-hanging tummy, muffin-tops, and puffy face, she could go a month without eating a thing.

But then she'd have no freaking breasts!

Cause breasts are always the first to go when you go on a diet!

It's just what every girl wants—freaking breasts freaking flat as a freaking pancake!

If you lined her up with most of the girls at school, she'd fit right in. Of course, you'd have to be careful what language you use to describe those girls. *Curvy features* is alright. *Full-figured*, not bad. *Heavyset, plump, chubby*, on the edge. *Plus size* works. *Voluptuous*, not bad. But you better avoid *obese*. And if you do use it, you better not add the word *morbidly* to it. And God have mercy on you if you ever utter the word *fat.*

"You're fat! fat! fat!" she says to the mirror.

But there are awfully slender and lovely girls in school, and Cindy Rand is one of that kind.

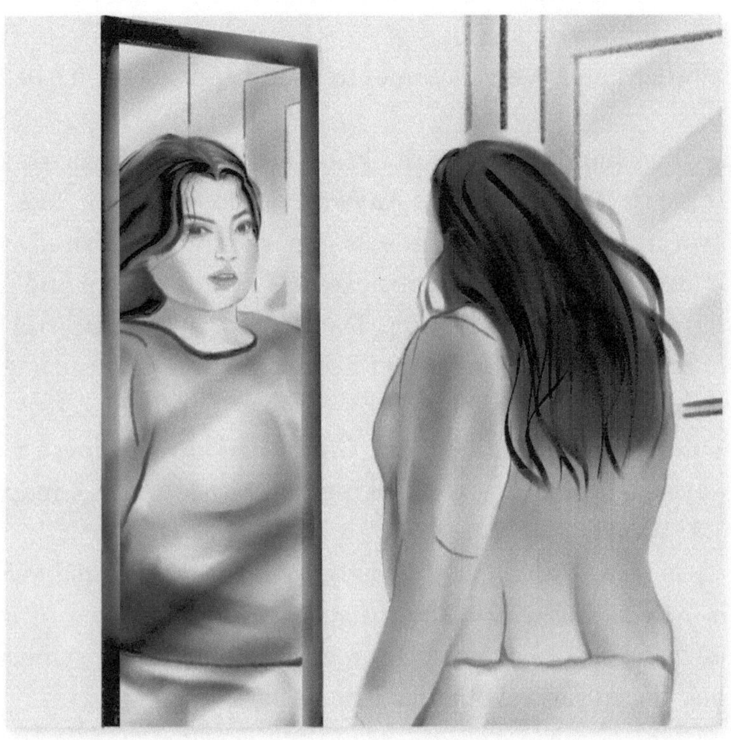

Cindy's in the eleventh grade and two years older, give or take, but lives only a block away. This explains why she and Dani started hanging out at the Stacy Ann Hastings Memorial Park swimming pool right after Cindy moved to Languishire from Tennessee. Dani was her best and only friend that summer. Cindy's a three-letter word nobody minds when you use it— hot. So why, after she'd gotten so many other friends and was two whole grades ahead of her, had she stayed best friends with Dani? Good question. Dani has to figure a way to rationalize it. Maybe Cindy's sketches—that *always* have slimmed her and beautified her—really do say how she sees her. Maybe Cindy means it when she says she has promise and could win beauty pageants. Cindy sure loved Silverdale, Harmony Mountain, and going sunning at Craggy Ledge. Maybe it's the mountain she likes.

But really, at the school dances when it's girl's choice, and when Cindy comes to ask her to dance, and when they dance, it's the older, prettier, and slender girl getting prettier, and the fat girl getting fatter! Not that she's complaining, but Cindy has a lot of other girls she could dance with. Why Dani?

On the other hand, when it comes to friendship, maybe it's better not to ask why.

On the other hand, Dani'd sure like to ask Cindy how she stays so slim, but the topic is too awkward. Anyway, it doesn't look like she does anything special. At school, she eats the same as everybody else and, besides swimming, her only serious exercise is jumping up and down as a cheerleader. When no one's looking, Dani does that, too. Up and down, up and down, making everything in her bedroom shake and causing Louie to think there's an earthquake.

But you'd never guess the *Dani* Cindy had drawn doesn't exist. Yet Cindy always said she does exist. Poking her with a finger, Cindy had said, *She's right there under your fat costume!*

Cindy also says, *With a face like yours, you have the potential to be queen of any beauty pageant you enter.* She insists Dani has the face of a glamour model and draws her to prove it. Dani especially likes her swimsuit drawings and has placed several of them around her room.

If only such an image were as easy to achieve as it is to draw! But she's tried many times to eat less, and nothing budges the needle on the scales more than a few pounds. And precisely where does she lose those few pounds from?

FROM HER FREAKING BREASTS, YOU FREAKING IDIOT!

On the other hand, how important is it to have breasts?

And, really, does she have to be as slender as Cindy?

On the other hand, Cindy sure knows how to draw faces, and every time Dani sees one of Cindy's conjurings, she stares at her own leaner face and those wistful dark eyes and that long black hair that cascades over her petite little supermodel shoulders and wonders if maybe it's true about her winning beauty pageants.

On the other hand, don't they have plus-size beauty pageants?

Now that the fat problem is solved, Dani sleepily goes back to the first problem—grocery shopping. Seeing that it's such an important job and that grocery stores aren't exactly familiar territory, she decides to wait till Saturday to make her debut pushing a grocery cart. Tomorrow's Friday. After school, she'll run over with her list, but only to pick up a few items like bread and milk and something frozen for tomorrow's dinner, then take a few minutes to check out the store and see about the cost of things.

That's when a new problem arises: Considering how long her list is, she thinks about the woman in the red cape. There's no way she'll be able to carry all that stuff home. You know, there's just never an easy solution to anything. She thinks and thinks, but, as always, sleep comes before solutions do.

7

His voice breaks the calm of the morning: "What are you doing?!"

It's a demand from Crazy Louie as he races his BMX bike up the driveway and skids his tire within inches of her feet. Dani jumps and screams. When she tries to slap his shoulder, he laughs and pulls away, making her look foolish.

She's parked his old Radio Flyer beside the house and stands there with the garden hose in her hand, tempted to spray him (but that would start WWIII). He takes on his usual bossy pose there, straddling his bike with crossed arms as she hoses black soot off the wagon.

"I'm going to use it to carry our groceries in, if you don't mind."

He watches as she uses soap and a brush to clean the filthy wagon—suddenly his most precious possession. He stands there and thinks and thinks. Then he says, "If you leave it parked outside the store, some homeless bum will steal it."

"Your name's written on it. See?" She shows him where long ago he'd used a knife to carve the letters L. Sentini. "Aren't all the bad kids afraid of you?"

She tips it and drains off the dirty water. This is the large metal model with the wooden racks. It was given to him for his birthday when he got a newspaper delivery job. But when he realized much of his profit came from tips, and how much work it required to earn those tips—like placing people's newspapers on their porches instead of their lawns, bushes, and roofs—he quit. She pulls the wagon by the handle around the driveway. The wheels still turn but sound like crows cawing.

Without saying any more, Crazy Louie goes into the garage and brings out an oil can. With this, he oils all four axles. It's the same oil can he uses for his precious bike. "Somebody steals it, you gotta pay for it," he huffs.

"What's it worth?"

He rattles off a fabulous number.

Dani scoffs. "What was it worth before I just washed it, when it was sitting in the corner loaded with a stack of junk, and you hadn't given it two seconds of your time for the last four years?" Crazy Louie considers this and she adds, "You know, you might want to be nicer to me from now on. I'm going to be in charge around here."

"Excuse me?"

"I'm taking on all the cooking, grocery buying, and money management. You'll be coming to me with your nickel and dime requests now. You'll be down on your knees begging for bubble gum money."

"I hardly think so."

"Ask Mom."

He scoffs and hawks and spits on the ground like the other boys do over around the half-pipe. It's disgusting, and she sprays the phlegm off the pavement. "You trying to be a pro baseball player, hawking and spitting everywhere? You're disgusting."

"You're disgusting," he says back.

But Dani doesn't back down. "I'm boss now. Super Boss. Big Daddy." She grins. "So you better stop spitting around here, cause I don't like it."

"You're big, alright."

"You're bigger," she retorts. "You're so fat you've bent the peddles on your little bike." He looks at his BMX with its sagging peddles. "Oh, I'm sorry," she says. "That's not cause you're fat. It's cause the bike was made for ten-year-olds to ride, just like your skateboard, which is sagging too, but only when you're on it. Cause you're a Fat Sister! Mario, Jimbo and Louieo! The Famous Fat Sisters of Languishire High!" She's relentless cause he asked for it. "By the way, can you still tie your own shoes?"

He uses one of his more vulgar expletives. "Can you still see your own p——y?"

It's a word, along with a host of others, which all the boys and some of the girls commonly use, some of them using the foul language in the halls right in front of teachers who keep walking, pretending not to have heard it—F words and B words and S words and MF words and, of course, the aforementioned P word. All of which are commonly heard on the rap music played everywhere on boom boxes like the kind they always have blaring around the pavilion at Stacy Ann Hastings Memorial Park.

But *she* now pretends not to have heard it.

It's a tune-out, she knows—the bigotry of low expectations. And it hurts her to do it. When she should step over there and slap his face for insulting her with such vulgarity, her silence actually does more harm; it puts her brother into the same category as so many of the boys at school whose parents, like Crazy Louie's mother, receive letters containing pamphlets that talk about how to handle kids at risk, signs to watch for, where to turn for help.

Worst of all, it isn't a word a boy of the mountains would ever use.

Judging by the way teachers turn their heads and do not see them, and turn their ears and do not hear them, one would have to conclude that half the boys at school fall into that category—AT RISK. There are AT RISK girls too—kids from whom most offenses are tolerated. But Dani doesn't consider herself one of them because she herself never does anything that would require *toleration*, nor does she say things for which anyone would need forbearance. She never uses the *lettered* words, nor even letters to replace the words with. For that matter, neither does Crazy Louie all that much. He's actually a good kid—except for moments like this when he freaking isn't.

On the other hand, Dani doubts if there are any of those kids who actually think they're AT RISK. The flash of this thought stirs her deeply as her brother suddenly seems to have lost whatever big-brother bully-momentum he had—having been reminded, by her cruel words, of his fatness; and, by her not slapping his face, of her low expectations of him; and, by the display of his like-new Radio Flyer, of his ineptness as a newspaper delivery boy.

Understanding, as Dani now does, that a new bicycle isn't exactly on the can-do list any more than will be a season ski pass at Sky Mountain in the fall, and feeling therefore some sympathy for the poor boy, she says almost cordially (and somewhat dishonestly): "If your wagon gets stolen, I'll pay you twenty bucks. I've seen them at garage sales for that."

"Never mind," he says. "You can have it." And he turns and sulks off, pushing his sad and rusting little BMX with its sad and sagging peddles into the sad and sagging garage, dragging his dirty old oil can with him.

Did she really need to mention the Fat Sisters?

8

Friday rolls around warmer and sunny. The light film of snow that was on the ground is gone, and there's only the brown, matted late-February grass and the gray trees, some of which are spotted with red buds anxious to pop open. The air is rich with loam, and it feels like spring. At the end of classes, with her short list in her pocket and wearing her toboggan hat and a pair of her Grandma Anita Sentini's knitted mittens, Dani sets out walking, heading from Crandall Street toward North Elm and turning south to walk the twelve short and familiar blocks to Main, then turning left and going past Maple to Central Avenue where Fletcher's Old-Town Market takes up a large space on the corner of Church Boulevard.

She had asked Cindy to walk with her and maybe give her some advice about grocery shopping, but Cindy Rand belongs to an art club which meets after school on Fridays, and she's been planning for the Easter Exhibition coming up. Lately, she and Cindy haven't seen much of each other. If it isn't the art club keeping her busy, or the Thespians, it's Jason Ashbakker, a topic that happens to be a rather fine thing to think about while walking down a chilly street.

Whenever Dani glimpses him in the halls and when he and Cindy eat lunch together, she gets jealous. Cindy knows it, too, although Dani has never mentioned how she feels because how exactly does a girl find herself feeling jealous over her girlfriend being too busy for her anymore cause she's in love with a freaking unbelievable hunk?

It was different in the old days at the beginning of their friendship. It was mostly Cindy giving her encouragement and support during the time when her mother left her father over his affair. That was when the two girls became like totally solid. In those times, they spent nearly all their time together, Dani finding it desirable to be out of the house, and Cindy's home being a kind of refuge, especially on weekends.

Part of it was her mother wanting her out—*away*, that is. You'd think her mom would have preferred to have her around. Maybe they could have comforted each other. But no, Crazy Louie spent most of this time at the Stacy Ann Hastings Memorial Park sharpening his BMX and skateboard skills and earning the name *Crazy*, while Dani fled the scene by almost living at Cindy Rand's home.

They were awfully good times if you didn't consider the break-up of her parents and the loss of her home when they moved to a crummy apartment. But maybe a bit bad, too. This was when she, Dani, began to see that Cindy wasn't the simple friend she thought she was. Well, to be more honest, it was she herself who wasn't as simple as *she* thought she was.

This topic has never been an easy thing for Dani to think about, much less discuss with anyone except Cindy, although for the life of her she can't imagine why. Feeling oneself attracted to such a perfectly gorgeous girl as Cindy Rand, who is older and wiser, seems like the most natural and easy and logical thing for anybody to do, whether they're a girl or not. Could somebody please explain why it's only boys who get to fall in love with beautiful girls? Perhaps what really mystifies her is why anyone, boy or girl, would feel attracted to *her*. But then that's easy to explain if you consider the comforts offered by such things as teddy bears, like hers she named Marco. Marco isn't exactly beautiful and doesn't exactly hug you back (he certainly doesn't kiss you back so you can't possibly practice kissing with him). Yet she's found him easy to love. He never judges her for the bad things she does just like she never judged Cindy for her bad things. Never once.

Speaking of discussing it, the topic came up by accident one Friday night—a Friday after one of the Thursday night dances in which Cindy and Dani danced close, and she found herself in a bit over her head. This was when the mood lights were dimmed extra low during a slow song by Roy Orbison. Somehow there came such a feeling of love inside her that she drew daringly closer to Cindy, and Cindy to her, and her eyes locked on Cindy's, and all of a sudden their lips came together. It hadn't been the first time, but it was the first time they'd kissed for real instead of for practice.

Later, she couldn't think of which of them had kissed the other. It just happened and it was magical. It was just like how she'd always imagined kissing Jason Ashbakker, or some boy of his equal. Mark Andichen was another. Arnie Laken. But this of Cindy, it just about curled her toes. And by Friday night she couldn't wait to sleep over with Cindy and figure a way to tell her how she felt.

Except that she couldn't tell her.

After a few awkward moments of staring at each other, it was Cindy who finally spoke. "Do you think we're in love?"

All Dani could say was, "I really freaking like dancing with you."

In the bedroom there, where they stood before Cindy's wide bureau mirror, Cindy stepped up and moved some of Dani's long black hair out of her face and smiled. "Do you know what I think?" Cindy's eyes kept flashing over her face, and she just glowed with excitement. "I think *we've* fallen in love."

The honesty of this confession raised her heart rate by at least a hundred beats. A moment passed before Dani could reply. In that time Cindy leaned in and kissed her again.

Dani had wanted to kiss her for a long time. That is to say, *honestly* kiss her. At Craggy Ledge, they'd sunbathed so many times and hiked and swam in Prism Lake, just the two of them, and so many times they'd fooled around, always giggling and saying it was for practice. Cindy liked to be Jason and to do pretend things.

"You have to practice at something to get good at it," she always said. But Dani said it, too.

Standing in front of the mirror, Dani was so blown away by Cindy's kiss tears began to leak from her and trickle down her cheeks. Cindy wiped them off with both her thumbs, but that only brought more. In a minute, Dani wept and had to put her fingers to her eyes, hoping to squeeze off the tears and get control of herself. Cindy wasn't a boy, but she was a living creature with a heart and soul, and Dani loved her.

"I don't know what else it could be?" Cindy went on with her thought. "But this is how I feel. Being with you makes me happy. It's like there's just love and nothing else. But with Jason, there's other things. It's complicated. Always takes up my whole brain to figure things out. But this is simple and real and perfect."

Cindy had reached into a drawer and pulled out one of her many sketches of Dani. This was one of those from an afternoon at Craggy Ledge. It was a certain place they liked to go way down among the big warm boulders where they were sure no one could see them. And they'd been sipping from a small juice bottle full of real wine Cindy had squirreled away in her backpack, and Cindy wanted her to pose for her.

She kept giving her instructions for the pose. It was supposed to be a sexy pose. Lean back, shift your shoulders a little this way. More. Now turn and look that way. But it was stupid to think anything she could do would be sexy, especially since her bathing suit was stretched nearly to the point of tearing. But when Cindy took her drawing pad and put her pencil to it, things had a way of improving. Her sketches somehow ascended to fine freaking art.

During the falling out between her dad and her mom, they'd all spent a lot of time in Silverdale, and Dani and Cindy had spent most of it together like that, and there had been a lot of sketches, even a few Cindy drew of herself, that she'd given to Dani.

Cindy showed her the drawing now—the one of sexy Dani. It was like the others Cindy had drawn of her—lovely and unbelievably of her in a fat-free pose! She'd seen them all. She had her own set of them, well hidden, of course, just like Cindy kept them hidden. And she, Dani, had begun to look at herself in mirrors and imagine herself somehow really fat-free and taller and as beautiful as Cindy insisted she was. But the big thing wasn't so much that Cindy had perfected her physically. That was obvious to see and for Cindy easy to do. But Dani felt perfected inside also.

It was as if Cindy had the power to change her really into a different girl.

Walking there, down Elm Street, as the noisy traffic passes on this cool late winter afternoon, she thinks of love and why Mary loved her little lamb.

Oh, wouldn't life be so simple if love could be that freaking simple!

9

The things she needs at Fletcher's Market are few today, and it would take her only a few minutes to get them, but Dani wants to look around. She wants to check out the store and see what kinds of things she can write about to fill up those five massive pages of her looming term paper. Five whole freaking pages full of words?! Won't it be like trying to fill up the Grand Canyon with Styrofoam peanuts?!

She grabs a small cart and begins walking up and down the aisles. She takes notice of all the varieties of everything and their prices. She's been in the store lots of times with her mother, but her interests were always limited to the snack and cereal aisles, the ice cream and frozen food freezers, and of course, the bakery. There had been one time recently when she'd found herself perusing the frozen yogurt shelves. Well, more than perusing. She had talked her mother into trying one kind after another, always selecting a brand that promised how eating yogurt was a good thing for weight loss. Then she figured out they aren't kidding when they say eating yogurt should be done in combination with a healthy diet and exercise. In other words, pretty much a general hunger strike combined with push-ups, sit-ups, pull-ups, and a blubbery jog.

But that's not such bad news in this case. Maybe she can fill a page with a lively story of her grand weight-loss failures.

As for *satisfying* meals, she's already perused her mother's recipe book, trying to come up with a few special dishes that might add more variety. After all, it is the duty of the cook to keep her diners wanting more. On the other hand, considering all the items required to make any one dish, she expects her grocery list will only get longer.

For example, there are things like sour cream, a variety of spices, a bag of flour, raisins, chocolate, cherries, blueberries, bananas, apples, a host of toppings and nuts, and many other things like that. So you always have to buy more than you need to make a single dish. That's going to require a kind of up-front investment. Added to this problem is the storekeeper's marketing tricks. On this, if you take advantage of the buy-one-get-one-for-half-price deals, you'll be buying much more than is needed for the week. That's why after making a few calculations in her head, she can see her sixty dollars won't be enough. To *save* money, she'll need *more* money. Hey, that right there is a freaking insight—the law of efficiency that Mrs. Kanbury talked about the same day she explained coupons.

Bingo, another page full of words.

She rounds a corner near the frozen food aisle, glowing in her new ease of academic stress, only to collide with another shopper's cart.

CLANG!

"Oh! I'm so sorry!" Dani looks up with big wide eyes and her fingers covering her mouth. "I'm so careless!"

"Excuse me!" says the woman in the red cape, her hood now turned down to reveal a head full of rich dark hair streaked with a touch of gray. "I have a bad habit of stepping in front of people!"

The woman's face is defined with the longer nose and cheek ridges customary to the Mediterranean bloodline. It's a glamorous kind of beauty that takes you by surprise when you notice the strands of gray hair. Besides that, ironically, it's Dani's own face aged by forty years.

That's cause Dani herself has a bloodline—one she doesn't think much about.

"It's me who should apologize," she says. "I wasn't paying attention."

The woman takes a quick glance at her cart and says, "You haven't anything in your cart, young lady."

"I'm checking out the store today, getting an idea about prices and things."

"Your first time shopping!" The red-caped woman cups her hand to her lips and more or less whispers: "Welcome to our little club of receipt collectors."

"Ha ha! Is that the game?"

"Oh, yes. And it lasts a lifetime. But you're starting awfully young."

"I'm here for a Home Ec assignment. I have to write an essay about grocery shopping and preparing a meal. But I'm also helping out my mom. Tomorrow's the big shopping day. Today I just wanna see what things cost. I think I'm gunna need to bring more money."

"Oh, well, you know, prices are quite distracting if you spend a lot of time thinking about them. I try not to." She laughs heartily. "When I was about your age, this can of soup cost ten cents."

"That must have been a long time ago," says Dani.

"Don't remind me." The woman adds: "But it seems like yesterday. Good luck with your essay."

Dani moves on down the aisle. By the time she gets the milk, eggs, cereal, some bread, and then tonight's frozen dinner, she sees the red-caped woman ahead of her in the checkout line. She waits her turn. She pays and places the items in a couple of plastic bags. Then she finds the bags quite heavy to carry.

Why didn't I go home and get the wagon first?!

She steps out onto the sidewalk where she sees the woman walking ahead of her. Then she hurries to catch up, placing both bags in one hand and walking crookedly like her grandpa used to do when he carried heavy pails of milk.

10

*D*anny calls out from behind, "How far do you have to go?"

The woman in the red cape stops and turns. "Hello again!"

Dani moves up to walk beside her.

"I live over on Morgan Street."

"That's my street," says Dani.

"Is that so? What number are you?"

"Three-O-four."

"I'm at seven-eleven, down near Hubbard."

"You've got a long way to carry that bag. And it looks heavy."

"It's not so bad. But I'm a bit worried about you. Yours looks heavier."

"I didn't realize a little bit of food could weigh so much." Dani now shifts one of her bags into her free hand. But the milk and bagels and pizza bag is way heavier than the cereal bag so she'll switch them shortly and give her tired arm a rest.

Food is so much lighter when you wear it, she thinks, and nearly laughs at herself for thinking it.

"Can I take something to lighten the load for you?"

"Oh, thank you. But these plastic bags make it a bit easier." Seeing that her new friend carries the paper bag with both arms wrapped around it, Dani asks, "How come you don't use plastic?"

"You'll laugh at my answer. I'm a little old-fashioned. But I like the old paper bags. I sometimes bring them with me and reuse them when I have quite a few saved up. I recycle them in different ways. I use them for recycling newspapers. You know what I heard once? Not sure if it's true, but I heard that if you use a paper bag, you help plant a tree. They say you're helping the forestry industry that plants more trees than it harvests. Besides, I really don't like plastic. A lotta times they tell you something's better for the environment, but it then turns out not to be any better than the other thing."

"I never thought of it like that."

The woman is walking at a good pace. Dani is thinking of the distance now and says, "You have to walk a long way to get home."

"I used to walk a lot farther than this to work every day. But thank goodness our city is small."

"It's still an awfully long ways," says Dani, feeling stress in her legs and shoulders already, taking longer strides than when she walks around the track at school. "Your arms must get awfully sore," she says, straining a bit and nearly laughing at the irony of her own arms getting sore.

"I switch arms at Elm, then again at Morgan, then again at Packer, which is right around your place. You know, it's awfully healthy for you to walk." As she says this, she glances toward Dani and shortens her gait enough to bring some relief.

"Once a week, I have to run two laps around the track at school," says Dani as her lungs work harder. "And that's quite enough exercise!"

"What's your name?"

"Dani. Dani Sentini."

"Ah! I recall that name might be from Sicily."

"Are you Italian? You sorta look Italian."

"I came from Sicily."

"You *actually* did?"

"Yes, actually," she laughs, "But it was my mother who came on a boat, and she brought me along in her tummy. Her mother and father brought her. But I've heard the stories so many times I feel like my feet were really on the boat, too. It's quite an honor to be a first-generation immigrant, you know. And quite another one to be Sicilian. If you're from Sicily, you can be awfully proud."

"I didn't know that."

"My Grandma used to tell me—she used to sit me down and tell me over and over again *if anybody asks you where you come from, you must never tell them Italy.* And when I asked why, she said *that's because your not Italian. You're Sicilian. And don't ever forget it.* Of course, my grandma did not speak English, and back then I didn't speak English too much either. The grand-folks, they really did not like to speak English or assimilate too much into American culture. But they loved America! And I think their pride came from when the American army invaded Italy in World War Two; and a big stage of that invasion was in Sicily. But us first-generation children and all generations after us, we were expected to become Americans and to speak very good English."

"Can you speak Italian?"

"Not much anymore. I don't use it enough. And English is quite a lot to handle, you know. And once I learned English and started learning a bit of history about America and the War, I began to be very proud to be born in America. I sure hope you're awfully proud to be an American."

"I know what you mean," says Dani. "A good thing you weren't born on the ship. Then what would you be?"

"Oh, I'd still be American. I don't want to be anything else. By the way, my name is Marian Natoli-Cantonia. A little hyphenation there for the sake of my grandma whose name was Natoli, a great and beautiful Sicilian name."

"My mom's mother, her name is Canale," explains Dani. "Which is also Italian, and some people pronounce it *Canalee.* My dad, though, he comes from a mix. His mother is Native American. She belongs to a tribe of the Northeast Tribes, among those who own Harmony Mountain. Her name was Rood. Anita Rood. And she married my Grandpa, Luigi Sentini. They live in Silverdale and own a farm at the foot of Harmony Mountain. If you remember it, it was the Federation of Tribes that had that big fight with the

United States Government back in the eighties. And kicked the government off the mountain."

"I absolutely remember it," says Marian. "I remember the story of those teenage boys who fought off the government guards and killed them. My heavens, what a story it was! And then there was a big show-down about the Federal Government trying to take over Harmony Mountain. Everybody thought there was going to be another Indian war. Even other tribes were moving in to help defend the mountain."

"Well, my Grandpa and Grandma were involved with that," says Dani proudly. "This research company who leased some land from the Northeast Tribes—it turned out they were trying to steal the mountain right out from under the Indian folk. But everybody knew it was the United States government that was really trying to steal it."

"You know, now that you mention all this," says Marian, "it's just another reminder how you can't trust your government. But, hey, you're a Native American. You already know that. And by the way, I can see a whole lot of your grandma in those high cheekbones of yours. And look at those jaws of yours. What a fine facial structure you have! Very remarkable, I must say. It gives you a certain elegance few girls have. And you know what? I've known a few Canales from Sicily. We might even be related, going back many generations. You could be a great, great, great-grand-niece—actual kinfolk!"

Dani chuckles. "So…alright! You're my aunt!"

"That's right. And I'm awfully glad we've finally met!"

"Say, I know a girl at school named Natoli."

"Oh, do you! That's another of my grand nieces! Maria!"

"Yeah, yeah! Maria Natoli."

"She's my brother's granddaughter, named after our grandmother. His name's Joseph, but most people always called him Joey. Joey Natoli. He still runs the bakery on the corner of Elm and South Main. My other brother, Carmen, started his own produce market over on Clayburn St. and Delaware Ave. Carmen's Fruits and Vegetables. And, of course, my father once operated a mechanics shop and fixed people's cars. His place was on South Main and Elm next to Joey's Bakery."

"My mom used to take us to Joey's Bakery," says Dani. We got donuts and cookies for breakfast. And I know another Joey who lives on Harmony Mountain. I was in love with him once. He's the grandson of Old Indian Joe, who is said to be the oldest member of our tribe and may be the oldest man on the planet. So maybe your Joey and mine are related," she adds.

"You're very cute."

"But *my* Joey was quite a lot older than me," says Dani. "So I don't love him anymore. But he had a younger brother by the name of Jay. Jay was more my age. I knew them once when they took me and my friend, Cindy Rand, on their motorcycles, but I had to ride with Jay and was jealous that I couldn't ride with Joey. Joey was so much finer!"

"I bet Jay's all grown up now and very fine indeed. I bet you'd prefer riding with him now."

Dani looks to her left and grins. "I hadn't thought of that. Do you know, these days I'd like riding on a motorcycle with any boy who'd take me, but I think I'd flatten his tires."

Marian politely changes the topic. "So...you had breakfast at Joey's bakery."

"Oh, yes. And my mom still gets her bagels there. She loves bagels and cream cheese, every morning. But I prefer the éclairs myself. But they're expensive, so I don't ask her to get them. But I've eaten a lot of them," she laughs.

"You know, that's not a very healthy breakfast—bagels and éclairs." She turns a sharp eye to Dani. "And Dani's a strange name for a girl."

"My name isn't really Dani. It's Danielle."

"I like Danielle. But I think—" Marian gives her a sideways look. "I think you're a Dani. You spell it with an i, don't you?"

"You're right."

Marian stops a moment and switches her grocery bag to the other arm. Dani takes that opportunity to do the same with hers. Then says, "And, say, if you'd like, I could help you carry your groceries. Since I live on the way to your house, how bout if I pick up my wagon and walk up to your place with you?"

"Oh, thank you. You're so kind. But you needn't bother. I'm quite accustomed to the walk."

"It's no bother at all. And in the future, maybe we can go to the market together and share the wagon. It's my brother's wagon from when he delivered newspapers, and somebody ought to use it. If we're related, I think that's the least I can do for my great-aunt."

"You're so awfully thoughtful. I think you must definitely be Sicilian and most certainly related also—and Native American no less! My great, great-grand something-or-other niece! To have finally met you! What wonders!"

They come to the big intersection of Elm St. and Marian pushes the cross-walk button.

11

he cars wait for them to cross Elm Street because they are slow and Elm is wide. They go straight on to Clinton, then to Morgan, turning left there and crossing Church Boulevard and continuing south on Morgan. Morgan Street is one of those old streets that goes by the old dark brown brick high school that's now a County Social Services office building on the corner of Clay and Helen. Marian says how she used to attend high school there and they used to have a principal named John Gaff who was over seven feet tall. He had to stoop to go into a classroom, and he used to take bad boys by their collars, two at a time if they had been fighting, and he'd drag them down to his office and nobody knows what he did with them after that but he had very few fights and nobody ever gave him backtalk.

"If he took boys by the collars today, he'd be expelled!" laughs Dani.

By this time they are approaching three-O-four where Dani says, "Would you come in for a moment while I put these away? Then I'll get my wagon. My arms are about to fall off and I bet yours are, too."

Dani turns now to cross the street and Marian follows. "Oh, this is awfully too much trouble for you, even if you are my niece!"

"It's quite a chilly wind," says Dani, going on. "Why don't you come in? I'll put stuff in the fridge and we'll be right on our way."

Dani goes across and Marian follows. "You're really awfully kind. Are you sure you have time?"

Dani hears her but is too busy thinking to answer. This lady in the red cape is awfully interesting and she doesn't want to let her go.

If I let her go, I might never see her again.

Dani goes up the steps and opens the door and holds it for Marian. They go in and she places her groceries on the kitchen table, then takes and sets Marian's bag on a chair. Through the living room door Marian sees Crazy Louie sitting there eating from a bag of corn chips and a jar of salsa, drinking a diet cola and watching *Seinfeld* on television. "Hello there," she says.

"This is Crazy Louie," says Dani. "He's my brother and unfortunately your great, great nephew."

Louie pulls his eyes away from the television and says, "Hi. What's going on?"

"This is Marian, our neighbor, possibly your great, great aunt."

"Hi Louie," says Marian. "It's nice to meet you after all this time."

"You might have heard his name mentioned on the radio," says Dani. "Crazy Louie Sentini. It's his BMX name. He's won several competitions down at the park. He has ribbons…and scars to match them."

"Goodness sakes! BMX, eh?"

"Bicycle motocross," says Crazy Louie. "And I never knew I had a great, great aunt."

"She's from Sicily like us. We're related. And I'm helping carry her groceries home," says Dani. "I'll be back in a few minutes."

Crazy Louie doesn't seem to have a clue about all this and just smiles like it's all a big joke. *Everything to him is a big freaking joke, anyway!* Dani goes on into the kitchen and Marian follows her down the hall where Dani puts the things away and stuffs her plastic shopping bags under the sink, poking and shoving them and closing the cupboard door quickly before all the compressed bags pop out.

"You have an awfully large kitchen," says Marian.

"It's very old," says Dani. "And there's hardly any space."

"It would make a fine kitchen, though, if anyone were to put in an island right where your dinette table is. What a beautiful space for an island—a big huge island with a sink and dining bar and a few stools!"

"We only rent it, so no one's gunna be putting in any islands any time soon."

"Well, remodeling kitchens takes a lot of money. I remodeled mine a few years ago. Whew!"

"Do you have an island?"

"I sure do! I said to my husband, if you build me a new kitchen without an island, I'll divorce you! And now, I can't imagine not having an island and a dining bar!"

"And an extra sink?" adds Dani.

"Yes! I told him that, too. An island, a bar and a sink or take a hike!"

"It sounds tropical."

"It is absolutely tropical! I'll show you when we get there. I'll make us some soup! We'll have us some soup at the lunch bar. We both need it after this walk."

"Well, we just use the table," says Dani.

"That's exactly what I had for the last forty years," says Marian. "A table just like that with the same upholstered chairs, but mine was a red set."

Dani knows Marian is just trying to be polite. All the counters are cluttered hideously, and so is the table. There's nothing you could call a workspace. "I'm going to be doing all the cooking from now on," she says. "So I'm gunna clean all this stuff off, and the dining table too, and then there'll be lots of space. I've got to clean out the refrigerator too," she tells Marian, seeing how Marian got a glimpse into it and it's pretty freaking bad, everything on top of everything else, and no doubt there's lots of containers full of leftovers rotten enough to kill a rat—perhaps things that haven't been opened in months, or years even.

Dani goes out, taking Marian's groceries in her arm.

"It was nice meeting you, Louie," says Marian.

Crazy Louie waves. "Goodbye, Aunt Marian!" he says as they go back out.

"That Louie, he cracks me up!" says Marian.

"Wait right here," says Dani, taking the groceries and heading to the garage where she places the bag in the Radio Flyer. She pulls the wagon out front, and she and Marian set out for number seven-eleven, four whole city blocks away, although Languishire is a small city, and the blocks tend to be short.

"I'm going to Fletcher's tomorrow morning," says Dani. "If you want to go with me, maybe there are a few things you need that are heavy. I've got quite a long list but only sixty dollars. Well, less than that now. So I'm pretty sure my wagon won't be very full. You're welcome to come along and take advantage of it."

"Thank you. You're so clever to use that bungee cord to keep the bag from falling over. It looks like a brand-new wagon."

"Crazy Louie didn't use it for long. He had a paper route. But he quit cause no one wanted to tip him, and his boss was complaining cause people weren't getting their papers delivered. As it turned out, he was riding his bike down the sidewalk and tossing the papers like a Frisbee, but he wasn't a very good shot. Many of them landed in the bushes or on the roofs."

"Is that why you call him Crazy Louie?"

"Oh, he's proud of that name. Everybody calls him that. It's like honorary. And if you ever saw him riding his BMX bike or his skateboard, you'd see why. He's really certifiably crazy. He's broken his arm, his wrist, and his nose, and he's gotten all sorts of stitches." Dani laughs and adds, "Some people even think he's the reason my mother works nights in the emergency room, so she can be there when he comes in."

"My heavens to glory!"

"Yeah, so he's earned that name and he loves it. He really is crazy."

"I can't imagine it. Surely you're exaggerating!"

"I assure you, I'm not."

They walk on down the street, crossing Packer, Delaware, and Washington, before coming to Hubbard. "I'm over there," says Marian, pointing to the large yellow brick and brown-trim house second from the corner on the left. They cross the street diagonally, and Dani looks up at the massive house and notices the eight mailboxes by the front door. She wheels the wagon to the steps and unhooks the rubber strap, but before she takes up the bag, Marian says, "Hey," and takes hold of her arm. "Let me show you something wonderful—a true promise of things to come!"

Marian leads her to the south side of the house, where she bends low and points to the violet and yellow flowers there. "Look at those!"

Dani draws near and bends low.

"Fresh crocuses! Five of them!" says Marian, highly animated with excitement. "Look at that would you! Take a good look! Proof there's no detail too insignificant for God's attention!"

The little flowers are hardly even visible, and probably most people would walk right by and never notice them, including Dani herself. But as she draws near, she sees what Marian is excited about. They certainly do look like spring itself, and Dani's spirits are lifted at the sight of them.

"Next, it'll be the forsythia, then daffodils, and tulips!" says Marian. "This house sure does love the spring! My husband helped me plant the gardens many years ago."

"It's an awfully beautiful house," says Dani, looking up. "And I don't know that I've ever even seen crocuses before."

"Oh, that can't be true."

"Well, I've never lived in a house where anyone would plant them."

"Maybe you just haven't looked for them."

"No, I guess I can't say that I have."

"Well, you should. You should look for them everywhere. Crocuses… you know, a lotta times they're like an echo from the past. Just think of it! Their brief little blossoms just popping up from the cold hard ground in March like that—because somebody wanted to bring a little joy into the world. You know, a lotta times the people who planted them are no longer with us. It seems so sad. Yet I feel so happy when I see them."

12

They go up the wide stone steps of the three-story house. There are masonry walls on either side of the stairs that curve wider to make a handsome apron, with curving iron handholds. The main entry door is tall, heavy, and dark. Marian goes in ahead of her to the foyer. The smell of the foyer is pleasant, suggesting somebody's baking. But there's also the smell of the old dark mahogany woodwork, but that's just lemon-scented Pledge which Dani has at home but never uses. Sometimes wood is just too freaking dusty to dust.

Altogether, these scents remind Dani of her Grandma Anita and the farmhouse in Silverdale—the many family visits on Thanksgiving, Christmas, Easter, and her grandfolks' special big Fourth of July barbecue. Her mind drifts on the sweet memories of all the things she took for granted once. Marian leads the way straight ahead, where she unlocks a tall door marked with #1 and enters. Inside is an even stronger aroma like you'd smell if somebody was baking a peach cobbler.

Dani hears the voice of Grandma Anita calling from the back porch telling them all to come in for dinner.

"Your place is beautiful," says Dani, standing still and looking all around the place. She toes off her shoes on the mat like she does at Grandma

Anita's. Marian does the same and leads her straight to the kitchen in the back, passing the doorways that lead to an elegant living room and an even more elegant dining room which features a sparkling swaggered chandelier whose hundred crystals refract the afternoon sunlight slanting through tall windows. The place is quiet.

"Hey!" says Dani. "I *love* your ferns! My grandma has ferns just like yours, and she says they're over fifty years old."

"Indeed! Boston fern can live a long time if it's cared for and its roots split up now and then with a bit of new soil thrown in."

A long and dark wood dining table stretches across the room and features ten side chairs and two arm chairs with maroon cushioned seats with plush velvet upholstery. Dani pauses to look in, noticing the handsome floor-length curtains with their stylish tan and maroon needlepoint. While many old houses have wood floors, here the wood is zigzagged. "I love your wood floor," she says. "I've never seen one like it."

"That's a parquet style, inlayed with dark walnut," says Marian proudly. "It's original to the house, if you can believe it."

When Dani turns back to the kitchen, she sees its marble counters that glisten in broad splashes of white and gray with green swirls that match the green of the ferns. And there's that island Marian mentioned, a broad and shining slab of marble with its own little sink with a tall looping faucet of brushed nickel like the ones she's seen in her mother's home fashion magazines.

"You sure weren't kidding about your island," says Dani. "It's gorgeous!"

"Thank you," says Marian. "I had the whole place remodeled eight years ago. You should have seen the old kitchen; it came all the way from the late forties when the house was converted into apartments. It even had an old porcelain-on-cast-iron sink with a faucet my husband had always to fix by replacing washers and seats. So I thought it about time for a facelift."

"Some facelift! Wow!"

"Sadly, he passed away before it was finished."

"Oooh . . . I'm so sorry to hear that."

"It was his smoking, I'm afraid. He quit, but not soon enough. It's best really never to start."

"Oh, I'd never consider it," says Dani.

"That's wise."

"So I take it you own this house?"

"Yes, actually. Mack and I saved our money and bought a few apartment houses back in the day. It was awfully difficult, but we made it through and finally paid off our debts. In fact, we had just paid off the last mortgage and hired a contractor for the renovation here when he passed away."

"That's so sad."

"Yeah, all those years of hard work and sacrifice, and he never got to see the rewards. The real irony is he remodeled most all of the apartments, saving our place for last." Marian looks around at the beauty of her kitchen, then adds, "You know, we always dreamed about the good life to come, the easy life, the *dream,* really. You always hear about the *dream*, right? But let me tell you, it takes so long to get there."

Dani looks around the place, taking in the fine kitchen like something she might see in a magazine, with all the fancy lights in the ceiling and the tiled floor and the cushioned stools at the island and the high ceiling and beautiful cabinets with crown moldings. As her eyes roam about, she notices the fine brass and white porcelain cupboard handles that feature a blue image of a tiny vine holding a bunch of grapes. She steps over to have a closer look.

"My husband designed those handles," says Marian. "We had them specially made and bought enough for all our kitchens. It's like a little trademark of his. Our own brand. It's awfully pretty on our letterheads. It's kind of nice to have your own emblem. A little pride never hurt anyone."

Having stashed all her goodies, Marian takes a can of soup from the cupboard, along with a pan. "Now, how about some hot soup? I've developed a bit of an appetite and it's well past time for a snack."

Dani looks at the clock, which says it's three forty-five. She must start supper at five, but the offer is so enticing she can't say no. "I'd love some soup."

Marian's house is so much like an actual home!

"Have a seat there and tell me about yourself. Would you like a glass of iced tea?"

"Uh, sure. That would be fine." But she'd rather have a diet cola.

"What's your mom and dad do?"

"My mother's a nurse at the hospital. She works evenings and has a second job in the mornings, so we don't see her all that much during the week."

"She's sure a hard worker. What about your dad?"

"My dad was in construction, but he got a herniated disk in his back and has been unable to work anymore."

"You know," says Marian. "I think I know your dad. His name's Angelo, isn't it? He runs Angelo's Construction Company?"

"Yup, that's him."

"He did some work for me one time. But when I asked him to work again his secretary told me he'd had an injury. But I never heard any more about him."

"Well, his back gave out. He was putting a ladder on his truck when it happened. Then they put in these metal pins and screws, but the pins slipped, and his back collapsed. He and his surgeon had some words, and I think he threatened to sue him. So that surgeon won't even see him anymore. He said Dad did things he shouldn't have done after he had the pins put in. When he went to find a different surgeon, nobody would operate. They say it's too risky. Could make him worse. But I think they're afraid he'll sue them. But I think he shouldn't have lifted heavy things after the pins were put in. And now he's stuck in a corner, not finding a surgeon to fix it, nor being able to work, and then having to take pain meds that he's gotten addicted to. He can't sleep without pills. He's like this legal drug addict and can barely walk or even think straight anymore. He can barely ride in a car. He has to have a special chair to sit in. He can't even lie down in a bed. He has to sleep in a reclining lounge chair that tips forward so he can stand up by himself."

"My heavens sakes. I'm so sorry to hear that. What an awful experience to have. How old is he?"

"He's like forty now," says Dani. "His disc broke about six years ago. Then the pins slipped about four months after his surgery."

"That's so sad," says Marian, pouring Dani a glass of tea and one for herself. "Are you able to care for him at all?"

"Not really. Before this happened, he got involved with the secretary of his company, and when my mother found out about it, she got mad and left. That's how come we live in an apartment. I didn't even know what happened. All of a sudden, my mother was on the rampage and we were moving out."

"What a shock it must have been!"

"I saw him a couple weeks later. He said my mother was never around anyway, and it was like he didn't even have a wife. He had to cook meals and stuff at night, after working all day at construction, and I helped, and so did Crazy Louie. He and I washed dishes and cleaned the house and stuff. But after we left, his secretary moved in. I mean, about a year later. So it wasn't so easy for us to just go over there, if you know what I mean. It isn't like a very homy place."

"Is his girlfriend still with him?"

"Yeah, she's running the construction company and stuff, but the work's gone way down. They're just barely making it. She has trouble finding good workers. Besides that, there's IsenellaFiber gone on strike, and everybody's wondering what's gunna happen."

"Oh, what a fiasco that is!"

"Yeah, and it makes everybody nervous. I mean, even if you don't work there, you worry. Cause there's been talk of business being slow. So it sets in a bad mood, you know."

"I've got some tenants who work there. They're very worried. And the ones I talk to didn't want to strike."

"Well, it's putting the breaks on business. That's for sure. I don't think there's too many around who'll be building new houses this summer or even remodeling. So he's like maxed out his credit, and insurance isn't paying very much. I mean, he has to pay so much before they pay anything it's like he doesn't even have any insurance. I don't think he could afford an operation even if there was a surgeon willing to do it."

"It's so sad these things. And such a shame about IsenellaFiber. Real estate people tell me their business is slow. Having such a big company in this little town—so many people with good-paying jobs and making so much money?! If anything were to happen, I mean, if they were to decide to close the plant, I think that's going to be very bad for the whole area."

"My best friend's father is production manager of that plant," says Dani. "She hasn't said they're closing. But I don't see her too much. She's too busy with her boyfriend."

"They have a place in Tennessee, you know," says Marian. "The workers should have thought about that before they voted to strike. If they close, they'll ship off their best workers down there. You can make tennis rackets anywhere."

"My friend says they've built a new plant in Mexico," says Dani.

"All I know is my tenants are worried. I've got four units supported by IsenellaFiber and I'm worried, too. And your dad's situation—what an upheaval for you all."

Dani looks up and gives this a moment to settle, then says something she's never confessed to anyone before, "At first I was very angry with him, when I found out about Margie Fuller. I said I hated him and never wanted to see him again. It was like, you know, maybe a girl has a built-in kind of disgust with men when they cheat, even if it's your father cheating. Like maybe it's just always gotta be his fault and in this case I think it was his fault. But I regret saying those things. I wish I could take it back."

"Love can be a complicated topic," says Marian. "You're not quite old enough to appreciate all the different ways it can get us in trouble."

Dani thinks of Cindy Rand. Her eyes dart away from Marian's. She shifts in her chair, and when she answers, she says something only a little childish ninth grader would say: "I don't think it needs to be. I think we just make it complicated. If people would just follow the rules, which are pretty simple. But my dad—with the help of Margie Fuller—he let himself be led down the garden path." These words come from her mother and nearly go sideways trying to get past her teeth.

"I hope you've forgiven him by now, hun. Adults have to face such conflicts. Sometimes I wonder how any of us get through it."

"I'm trying to. And Margie as well. She's awfully nice. I mean, I like her alright. But did she have to take him away from Mom and us? Couldn't she find a guy of her own?"

"If only love could be so easy as that."

"What I can't figure out is why my mom's so friendly with them. She goes over there all the time. She's friends with Margie. She even pays for a lot of his meds. I think I'd be awfully angry if I were her."

"With a little more experience, you'll begin to see things aren't so black and white," says Marian. "I think there's always a little blame to go around. None of us are pure if we're honest with ourselves. You're much too young to know what it's like to love someone you shouldn't."

13

*I*t's a conversation Dani would like to have—about loving someone you shouldn't. For reasons she can't explain, it seems that Marian Natoli-Cantonia from Sicily would be a good one to ask. But this isn't a good time, so she lets it drop.

And Marian says, "So now it's come time for you, taking over some of the cooking and things for your mom?"

"That's about it. I asked her if I could, cause we never have any food in the house. It's like twenty bucks here and twenty bucks there. There's so little food I wonder how I coulda gotten so fat. So I suggested maybe I should take over the cooking and grocery buying and then I wanna start managing all our money. I think I can do it better than she does. She has no time. Besides the hospital, she works at Ozzie's Diner from nine to two-thirty. Then she comes home to prepare our dinner and goes to work leaving instructions for me to cook it. But it's usually just a frozen dinner like a pizza or a frozen stroganoff. She gives us money for take-out food like KFC, but that's a long bike ride up on North Elm Street."

"When does she get a good night's sleep?"

"On weekends when she's not on weekend duty. But she's almost always on weekend duty. She's like the best nurse in the ER. And she's always called in for complicated surgeries. And I have to say, not to defend my dad for what he did, but the truth is my mom likes being at the hospital. She's always going in for more hours any time she has a chance to. She was always like that."

"So you weren't really at the store for a Home Ec paper, were you?"

"Oh, I have that, too. Why not do both?"

Marian laughs. "So, you're what, sixteen?"

"I wish. I'm fifteen. I'll be sixteen June twenty-first, the day school lets out for summer."

"You look so much older than fifteen."

"That's cause I'm fat."

"Oh, don't be harsh on yourself! You're a bit overweight. Nothing a better diet and exercise won't cure."

"Ha! I've tried diets like you wouldn't believe. Thanks for being kind, but I'm finally facing the truth. Obesity's in my destiny! Cause it's in my genes."

"Now, *that's* going too far. Obesity!" she scoffs. "And I don't believe all this about fat genes! None of my grandparents were obese. Were yours?"

"I weigh a hundred and eighty-five pounds, sometimes one-ninety. I'm inching up. But really, I should only weigh one-fifteen. But I'd like to get down to one-ten."

"One-ten?! You'd be a skinny girl at one-ten! You're tall. And I'm sure you're still growing."

"One-fifteen tops, only cause I'm tall. I can't even fit into my mirror." Dani laughs. "It's true. I've got to go out and get a bigger mirror. I'm wider by a foot!" Dani squeezes the sagging pouch of fat above her hips to show Marian how fat she really is. "That's just plain disgusting!"

It's also truly vulgar cause Crazy Louie was right! The answer is a big fat NO! She can't see her freaking you-know-what!

Marian has taken a tall candle from off the dining table and placed it on the island bar before them, lighting it with an igniter. She then proceeds to make up some canned chicken salad sandwiches on rye bread, slicing them diagonally, and pours each a bowl of steamy tomato soup. When she sits down beside Dani, she bows her head and closes her eyes for a brief moment, then takes up her spoon.

Dani has all she can do to keep from wolfing down the sandwich. Perhaps it's the fine setting or Marian's patient approach to her own food; maybe it's the candle, but Dani finds herself following Marian's lead and taking little bites of the sandwich wedge and sipping her soup slowly. Maybe it's that she likes spending time with Marian, and eating slowly is a way to prolong it.

While they eat there at the island, sitting side by side on tall stools, she manages to tell Marian quite a lot about herself, even telling her more about Cindy, describing her as an older and wiser friend from the neighborhood, and how Cindy, as an artist, likes to draw her in all these different poses and what she says about how she, Dani, could win a beauty pageant.

"Of course, Cindy's just being kind," says Dani. "She's always drawing me minus about fifty pounds. It always makes me feel so much better and really confident, right up until I look in the mirror and see the truth—which is that I'm fat. And that is that."

Dani seems to talk on endlessly, finding Marian to be a good listener in a world where there are few of them. As she talks, she begins to notice how slender and attractive Marian is for her age. Her figure is petite, and her face seems radiantly healthy, as if she has a bit of a natural tan. She's especially pretty with her narrow nose and those soft brown eyes. Her tall forehead rising to the line of her black hair gives her a certain elegance. As Dani takes more careful notice of her, she can see that while Marian is really quite pretty now, in her youth, she had to be a solid beauty.

Suddenly, she says to her, "Oh, my word! That photo on the wall by the door there—that's you?!"

"Yeah, that's me, alright." Marian chuckles and smiles modestly. "I was twenty-two and crazy about dancing and boys. Already much too experienced with reality. A bit like you, actually. I got married in 1968 when I was seventeen to a gorgeous boy who was being shipped off to Vietnam. He never came home. I loved him so much, and I cried for two years. Then I married another man in 1971 who was likely to be drafted too, but the draft lottery saved him. Mack was a real go-getter sort of guy who had all these ideas about buying houses with apartments. He was handsome and thought I was too. I was attending a two-year business college, and when I graduated, I went to work at the National Bank.

"Mack was working for a contractor," she continues, "building houses up in the Heights. He and I pooled our money and began to buy houses, thinking it was a good way to shelter some of our money from taxes and then maybe to have a little extra so we could afford to send our kids to college one day. Some of the houses were single-family places, some were duplexes, and some were like this house that has eight apartments. We liked this house so much we moved in and have lived here ever since. I liked the high ceilings and tall windows, and he liked the carriage house. We had four children and raised them right here. It looks small, but it has four bedrooms, one downstairs and three up. Ours was the big bedroom in the back with its own bathroom. The carriage house was his shop. Over the years, we've managed to acquire seven more houses for a total of thirty-five apartments. I managed them and rented them, and he took care of them and fixed them up."

"So you both could have regular jobs and have apartments, too?"

"For a time, we both worked. Had to. We were never rich. I worked at the bank as a teller. I managed our apartments in my spare time. We owed a lot of money in loans and mortgages. Our monthly payments and expenses were so high we had to scrimp to make ends meet. It was quite a struggle if someone couldn't pay their rent, so we had to be careful to choose good tenants. Fortunately, I'm a pretty good judge of character and didn't make too many mistakes."

"What about Mack?"

"Like I say, Mack worked for a home builder. He didn't have any special craftsman talents but was a reliable worker and paid attention to details. He never took days off, he came to work on time, and he wasn't afraid to get his hands dirty. He had the talent for looking ahead and seeing what needed doing and going ahead and doing it without somebody having to ask him. He was doing well and making pretty good money, but gradually began to devote all his time to remodeling our apartments and doing a few remodeling jobs for others on the side. Kinda doing what your dad used to do."

"Did you have health insurance?" asks Dani.

"That's quite a strange question for a girl your age to ask."

"Unfortunately, I know a bit too much about insurance. It's been a big topic of conversation since my father's injury. His insurance has a very high deductible and the premium still costs a lot. So his bills have been adding up so high he doesn't think he'll ever be able to pay them."

"That's another reason I stayed working for the bank," says Marian. "I had good health insurance that covered Mack and the children. It's another reason to think twice before you go off with your secretary. You know, Dani, we're all fragile. It's wise to have circumspection about life. When you think about it, life is pretty short, and near as I can tell, most everyone who lives down here in Realityville is hanging by a thread when it comes to finances. That's why it's a good idea to think about your future when you're young. Take in the bigger picture of things. Believe it or not, that's especially true when you're young. You should start as soon as possible to follow a long-term plan for your life; and ours happened to be a plan for independent wealth. We just didn't think it was a good idea to depend on somebody else's success. I'm not saying that's the best plan for everyone. But everyone healthy enough to work can do it. That's the most important thing. If you want real financial security, you need to start when you're young and try to focus on projects that will build your personal wealth. Even at your age. It's not too soon for you to be thinking about it. Time flies by so fast, and pretty soon you'll wonder where it went."

"I'd sure like to know how to do *that!*" says Dani. "I mean about the wealth. I sure could use some advice."

This last thing Dani says without really expecting there to be a very useful answer. But Marian surprises her.

14

arian takes a moment to consider Dani's comment. "You know, Dani, this is the very first time a young person such as yourself has ever asked me that question."

"Who wouldn't want to know?"

"I never thought much about it. I mean, as a thing to teach. Our own children grew up in a home where all our focus was on living frugally, saving all the money we could, and investing it in real estate. Just about everything we did in our day-to-day lives was oriented one way or the other toward building wealth. It never occurred to me that someone might not know how to do that. I guess we took it for granted that our own children knew how by observing how we lived our lives."

"Well, I honestly have no clue," said Dani. "In fact, I can't even imagine how anyone actually saves money and builds wealth. But the living frugally part, I do know about that pretty well. So, if I may ask, are your children wealthy also?"

"That word *wealthy* can be tricky," explains Marian. "It needs explaining. But to answer your question the way you meant it, the answer is no. My children are not wealthy. But all of them have chosen paths that will eventually lead to their financial security."

"You mean, they're *getting* rich."

"No. Not at all. That's not what the word *wealthy* means. At least not to me. To me, the term *wealthy* is used always in the term *independently wealthy* or when you say someone is *financially secure*. That can mean you're rich or it can mean that you have sufficient outside income of your own so that you don't depend on the government or someone else's business model to provide your paycheck. It might mean you own a retail store and work for yourself, like my brother Joey and his bakery, or my brother Carmen and his vegetable stand.

"But it's even more than that," Marian continues. "Merely having a store doesn't guarantee financial security. Joey and Carmen also invested in real estate as a store of wealth. Carmen took his money and bought several apartments, and Joey bought land along Cutter Lake, built a cottage, and then built a few more and now rents them by the week as summer vacation rentals. His land is extremely valuable today."

Dani listens intently as Marian tells the story.

"My father wasn't close to being rich, but he became independently wealthy through his auto repair shop, which he bought, along with the land beside it. And his foresight to buy that land provided his retirement when he sold it; and it gave him the funds to pay for my business courses.

"You take a place like Fletchers Market, for example," continues Marian. "The Fletchers own the grocery store, which is independently owned and managed. I mean, it's not a chain store like a lot of them. But I've been told they also have a profit-sharing program for their employees. That's what every employer should do. But for the Fletchers themselves, maybe someday the store will close because of competition from the bigger chain supermarkets, but the Fletchers own other commercial and residential rental properties. It's never a good idea to keep all your eggs in one basket."

"Does profit-sharing make the employees of Fletchers independently wealthy?"

"No. But it puts them in good stead to save their profit-sharing and convert that into a store of wealth, like real estate or the stock market. To build wealth, you must take your inert savings and invest it into an appreciating asset—ideally something that produces income."

"I sure wish the hospital had a profit-sharing program for their employees," says Dani. "When you think about what people pay for health care."

Marian laughs. "Well, you know, they're non-profit."

"Yeah, but their administrators sure aren't. They're rich! Mega rich! A lot of them live in the big houses in the Heights and have fancy cars and swimming pools."

"Well, there's a goal for you," says Marian. "Perhaps something in medical administration."

"That's like saying I want to grow up to be a corporate president. Yet you're richer than they are," says Dani. "Considering you own thirty-five apartments. If you're getting two thousand a month from each one, then you're taking in about seventy thousand dollars a month. I'd say that's rich. If you wanted, I bet you could live in a castle in the Heights with a big swimming pool, too."

Marian laughs. "Don't I wish I was actually making that much! You're forgetting about the expenses, my sweet. There are taxes, insurance, utilities, and quite a lot for maintenance. And most of all, don't forget about the replacements—that's remodeling, renovations, roofs, and things like boilers and furnaces. You notice all my windows here are new, and they're new at most of my houses. That's a lot of money. Fact is, I couldn't afford to live in the Heights if I wanted to. Besides that, my car's getting old—well, actually it *is* old. Owning rental properties takes a lot of money, dear, and a lot of time. You know what it's like? I'll tell you. It's just like being a farmer."

"But you're the landlord. You own them. And you said you've paid off all your debts."

"Yes. That's true. After forty years of worries and stresses and penny-pinching, I not only own them, but my husband and I have remodeled most of them. However, while I'm retired from the bank, I'm not retired from my apartment business. So, while we may look rich on the surface, Mack and I didn't get rich. We became independently wealthy by providing a service that people need—the service of providing nice, high-quality housing. And by the way, I don't like the name *landlord*. There's not much *land* involved with it, and there's certainly no *lords*. I prefer to be known as a *housing provider.*"

"What about your kids? What do they do?"

"My oldest daughter, Natalie, is an accountant. She has her own office and a staff of three. My youngest son, Mark, is an architect. He doesn't have his own office, but he's working toward that goal. My youngest daughter, Francesca, is a real estate broker, and she may be branching out on her own, but in that profession, you're always an independent operator even when you work with a brokerage firm. And my oldest son, Tommy, is helping me with the apartments. He spent a lot of time working with his father and seems to like apartment work, which involves a lot of different things from painting to carpentry and a lot of special projects like installing new kitchens and bathrooms. Tommy's quite talented and well suited to the art of *housing provider*. It's quite a challenging occupation and demands a variety of skills. It isn't for everyone."

At this point, Dani is feeling a bit overwhelmed to take all this in. Marian stops talking and asks her, "Dani, tell me about a few of your goals."

"Ugh-oh. Answering that always gives me stress," Dani laughs.

They'd both finished their soup and sandwiches, and Marian pours more iced tea. Dani finds the unsweetened tea bitter. How can anybody drink anything unsweetened? She sits back in the stool there, watching the candle's flame, and considers her goals. It isn't that she hasn't thought about goals so much as that no one has actually asked her to speak them aloud. Goals are better left down deep inside where she keeps her secrets and her dieting plans, and of course, where she can cancel them without anyone noticing.

"When I was a child growing up," says Marian, "there were a few years where I worked with my mother at a farm a little ways from here that hired itinerant help to pick produce. They had lots of different crops, and during harvest time, you could always go up there and get a job. There were apples, peaches, cherries, strawberries, sweetcorn, and lots of string beans.

"So I helped her pick all kinds of things—I loved the peaches most of all. Not that you could eat them. They weren't even ripe. But they were fun to pick. And she arranged for me to be paid some small amount. I might have been ten or twelve at that time, but I was a good picker. I think I made something like four dollars a week, but they were different times and everything cost less. I thought it was a lot of money for me to be able to earn to help my parents. But you know, at that time, I had great dreams of one day becoming a dancer. I had visions of myself as a cabaret dancer of Hollywood caliber. But it wasn't the dancing itself I dreamed about, nor the fame, but really I just wanted to be beautiful."

"Did you ever dance? I mean, for money?"

"I did, actually. Quite a lot, in fact. But not so much for the money. I eventually became a dancer with a bundle of ribbons for winning competitions. But it was only the local dance halls like The Four Leaves and Highlights where they had the contests with prizes. I usually won those contests and I collected a lot of blue ribbons and that photo on the wall is of me winning one of them. So you could say I achieved at least one of my goals."

Dani stands and goes to the photo to get a better look, noting that Marian's goal to become beautiful was attained in spades—her slender figure, the beautiful face, the kind of legs to freaking die for.

"I think I have a similar goal," she says, taking her seat again.

"Dancing?" says Marian, her brow rising in surprise.

"No, the other part. It makes me think about my friend Cindy's drawings of me. I think if I could name one absolute goal, it would be to really become the girl she seems to see when she draws me."

"Oh—the winner of a beauty pageant!"

"She's awfully nice to say it."

"Well, I can see why she says it. Your face has all the indications of your fine genetics—a Sicilian grandfather mixed with Native American blood? How could you not be glamorous? So, I'll just go ahead and say it, then. I too think you could be a beauty queen. I have no doubt you'd make it big in Hollywood, but only if you'll lose that extra weight."

"Wouldn't *extra weight* be something on the scale of a paper boy's bag full of Sunday newspapers?"

"In fact," adds Marian ignoring her, "I could just about guarantee you have a potential for enormous glamour—the kind they put on the covers of magazines. Your eyes are sharp and beautiful, your face is long and very Mediterranean—a little something with your hair, a bit longer maybe, knock off those extra pounds, tone up maybe with a bit more walking and good old-fashioned exercises—yeah, I think I could guarantee it. For sure you'd be the most beautiful girl in Languishire."

As a wide smile spreads over her face, Dani feels herself go nearly weightless sitting there. It's like she's stepped through one of those spirits they say are always drifting around Harmony Mountain; and if you pass through one, you might find yourself flying above the earth like an eagle.

15

hinking about being beautiful is enough to set Dani soaring with the eagles, while a little moment passes.

"But having beauty can't be your only goal," adds Marian. "We girls are like flowers. Beauty fades long before the eyes that see it."

"Yours hasn't," says Dani.

"Oh, don't be silly. Youth is but a brief moment in an all-too-short life."

At the risk of appearing materialistic, a word her mother uses every time Dani wants something that is actually materialistic, Dani reaches in a bit deeper and drags out a not very noble goal. "Besides that, I do think a lot about what it would be like to be rich," she says.

"Don't we all!"

"Did you ever? I mean when you were picking beans and cherries? Did you dream of one day having a house like this?"

"It was a bridge too far to ever dream of owning a house like this. When I married Mack and we decided to buy the houses, our goal was only to earn extra money to put our children through college. We never dreamed of becoming rich. Like I've already said, we were definitely not rich. I am not rich now. Although we didn't plan for it, what we achieved was what I already explained. We did become independently wealthy. I didn't know enough back in those times to have such a goal as that, but I think that's a goal everyone ought to have."

"But everyone can't buy apartments," says Dani. "We need people to be doctors and dentists and bankers and writers and musicians. You know, factory workers can't be independent."

"That's not true. There are many different vocations. And you must pursue yours. But whatever field of work you choose, it is possible to become independently secure. Even a factory worker can invest and have a store of wealth. For example, a factory worker could afford to buy a home. But he or she can also afford to buy a duplex—a simple little house with just two apartments. This is easier to do than you might think. One way to do that is to buy a duplex to live in yourself. It's a great source of income, the rent helps pay the mortgage, and it provides an income tax shelter. I'd highly recommend such an investment for any factory worker, even if it's only one duplex. But why not save up and buy another and another? I've even suggested this to quite a few people over the years, and a few of them actually went out and did it. They're very happy they did. I bet—I mean, I don't know your mom, of course—but I bet it's something she could do."

"Buy a house?" To Dani, this concept is just too dreamy to take seriously.

"Yeah, sure, with an apartment or two. You know, the rent helps pay the bills. The income tax shelter is a big deal."

A moment later, Marian asks a good question: "Could I ask, Dani, do you know why your mom rents your house instead of owning it?"

"Because she left my father. She was so angry, she moved out, and we went with her. I don't think she had much money. So she just rented any old apartment, and that's where we live."

"Sometimes, Dani, I think the problem is as simple as not having enough information to make a wise decision. People are really not very well educated on the topic of saving money and investing."

"You mentioned a tax shelter. What's a tax shelter?"

"It's a way to save a little bit on your income taxes by deducting your expenses from your income. You know, the less you make, the lower your taxes are. And there's another advantage—you can depreciate the rented space of your home, and, by doing that, reduce your taxable income even more."

"How do you do that? What's *depreciate* even mean?"

"With income taxes, it means to reduce the value of your real estate a little bit every year and deduct that amount from your income, in this way reducing your tax obligation. It can be a bit complicated. Maybe some other time. If you're really interested, I can explain it to you. But deducting certain expenses and depreciation lowers your income taxes."

Suddenly a thought comes to Dani and she says, "You know, we really need nurses. And my mom's a nurse. But there's no way she could be independently secure like you. Working two jobs still leaves her with little left over. There's no way she could do what you did."

"Having a little left over is all you need. A little adds up to a lot eventually. You'd be surprised what a little can do for you over time. That's how banks earn their money—incrementally through interest payments over a long period of time."

"It sounds like a bridge too far to us," says Dani.

"A lot of people think that way. That's why there are so few owners and so many renters."

"I really don't think my mother's cut out for being a landlord or running any kind of business. But she's a good nurse. And the world needs nurses. So I'm pretty sure she'll always have to depend on the hospital for her income."

"You know what," says Marian. "I think your mom is already independently wealthy. Just consider that she could enter private nursing. I know a girl who's a private R. N. and she does quite well. A lot of times, being independently secure means you have a set of skills that are in high demand and those skills can be taken with you wherever you go. In my opinion, that's independent wealth—when you develop indispensable knowledge and skills. That's as good as what Mack and I accomplished. And it's true, not everyone is cut out for running their own business. Being a housing provider has its challenges, and that's putting it mildly."

"That sounds awfully nice, and you're nice to say it. My mom may be able to take her skills all the way to the moon, but that hasn't put marble on her kitchen counters nor crystal in her chandeliers. If you looked in her pocketbook, you wouldn't exactly sing praises to her independent wealth."

Marian pauses and takes a moment to study Dani's face. Then she says, "Dani, you know it's true in life that not everyone is cut out to be *independent*. Maybe most people aren't. It's not easy to achieve—running your own business, like apartments or a fruit stand or a bakery. These enterprises require a certain entrepreneurial spirit. That means they must be willing to live a life that's not always safe from risks and setbacks. I think most people really prefer to have ordinary jobs that do not have the stress of business risks. They're taking risks, of course, because the company they work for might go out of business, and then they'd lose their job and have to find another. But at least they get to live most days free of the constant stresses that come with independence. They get to take vacations and don't have to make sure somebody's watching the farm.

"Freedom isn't really free, you know," Marian continues. "There's a price to be paid for it. When I look around, I'm beginning to realize most people don't value freedom so much anymore. They'd rather have an easy life *today*, a life free of responsibility where there's no need to make sacrifices or take risks. I think more and more people are being trained to be dispensable and easily replaceable and to throw off the duties that come with personal accomplishment and excellence and achievement, all of which require a certain desire to be in some way superior to the average others."

"Seems like at school we're mostly taught that everybody's equal," says Dani. "Nobody's exceptional. Nobody's inferior, and nobody's better. That's why they always put us in *working groups*. No one person gets credit. They all get credit, even the ones who don't do any work. So what's the use trying to be excellent or superior if there's no benefit in the end? I hate to work in groups."

"I'm glad you feel that way. Shows you have an independent spirit. No matter how hard they try to snuff out your individuality," says Marian, "they will fail because nature always rewards strength and punishes weakness. There are rules that can't be broken. The key is to know those rules and use them to your advantage."

"I'd sure like to know how to do that."

"Well, take me for example. I never went to actual college, only to that business school that my father helped pay for. And since I was thinking along the lines of business, and specifically the banking business, I was alerted one day when I saw an advertisement in the newspaper for a five-day seminar that offered to teach the skills of success. I thought it strange—the idea that success could be taught like math or English. I thought success came automatically from scoring well on the exams. But this was a special course that simply taught you how to *behave* successfully and employ certain techniques that successful people are especially good at. So I asked my father for more money, and he gave it to me. My father was very confident in me, always assuring me I could do anything I set my mind to. And do you know, when I signed up to take that seminar, there were only thirty people there out of a whole city? Wouldn't you think, a seminar on how to be successful, shouldn't the whole city have been there?

"And wow! How amazed I was at how using those techniques changed my life. I became a much more effective teller at the bank and was quickly promoted to a branch manager and then to vice president of public relations. It's a title that brings a lot of prestige with it. And I must say, there are very few bank vice presidents who've never been to college. But I didn't get there merely because of what I knew about banking. I was successful because I used the common techniques that are guaranteed to result in success."

"How about sharing a few examples?"

"Well, you already know a few of them. For one thing, you're hungry to learn and seem to be a good listener. For another, you're willing to help others. And one of the most important keys to success is—guess what?—smiling."

"Smiling?"

"Yes, smiling, even when you're on the phone. The very act of smiling gives one an emotional lift of confidence that resonates in your voice and will have a positive effect on others. Here's something for you to do. Next time you're someplace where there are a lot of people, look around and notice if anybody's smiling. I think you'll find very few are. But *you* do it.

You smile a lot. I noticed it right away. And since I met you, you've been smiling about every minute. You smiled even when our shopping carts collided. But I especially like it when you smile as you're talking about your friend Cindy Rand."

But now Marian glances at the clock. "Hey, it's almost five-thirty! I bet your brother Louie's getting hungry."

"He's always hungry and he's always eating."

"Do you have a shopping list for tomorrow's big grocery day?"

"I have it right here. I brought it with me to the store."

"May I see it?"

Dani digs it out of her pocket. Marian opens the folded page of notebook paper and her eyes begin to follow down the list. After a moment, she says, "Dani, I want to give you some advice here, but I don't want to offend you. Are you able to accept advice? I mean, are you able to step outside of your bones for a moment and look with an objective view at your situation?"

"What's that mean, an *objective view?*"

"As if you were someone else looking down from high above, without having already formed any conclusions, and you could be free to choose any way forward, sideways or backward, no matter what it is?"

"I don't know if I have formed any conclusions, except what I see as the obvious."

"Well, sometimes we can be overly harsh on ourselves, and this can make things worse than they are. Some people are defeatists. Defeatists believe they are defeated and so, in fact, they intend to be defeated no matter what. Others tend to be the opposite, convincing themselves they're on the right path and nothing's going to turn them off it. There's a middle ground where a person can take constructive criticism and find a way to take that advice and convert it into positive actions."

"You know, I don't think I've ever had any criticism except for the kind Crazy Louie gives me, and I give it right back in doubles."

"I think Louie may not like to be called by that name."

For an instant, the conversation stops. Suddenly, there's a gap in the flow of the moment.

"He seems to like it alright."

"A name is awfully important, Dani. And nicknames can be hurtful if they define a person negatively, and a lot of times they do. Isn't *Louie* itself a nickname?"

"Yeah, actually, his name is Louis. But how can a nickname be hurtful?"

"Well, we all grow and change. But a nickname like Crazy Louie is like a lock on a certain time in your brother's life. You said he's had that nickname since he won bicycle competitions when he was a boy. That's quite a long time ago for him. Louis is getting older and may be ready to put the old things of childhood behind him. He's most likely getting tired of always having to live up to the standards of *crazy*."

Once they are spoken, Dani can see the words are true.

"But that's not what I wanted to advise you about," says Marian. "How about if I go to the store with you tomorrow? Would you like some company? I'll go over your list tonight and make a few suggestions that might help you achieve a few of your goals."

"I'd love it if you would. Why don't you stop by my house around nine? We'll walk down to the store together."

"Also," adds Marian, "if you'd like me to, I can give you some tips about nutrition. I've gotten a few books on that topic and I've picked up a few things from my sister Teressa. She's actually a nutritionist at the hospital. And I've read lots of diet articles in the newspaper. It's pretty amazing how much info on dieting you can find right in your newspaper."

"I'd love to know more about it."

"It's quite an important topic. I'll see you in the morning and we'll talk more about it."

<h1 style="text-align:center">16</h1>

ani comes into the kitchen through the back door after putting the wagon away. When Crazy Louie comes in from the living room, it's like a galactic collision.

"Don't bother making supper," he says, steamed. "I've already eaten. And why aren't you answering your phone?!"

"It's only five-thirty. We usually don't eat till then."

"It's five-forty-five!" He points to the clock.

"That clock is ten minutes ahead of time, and you know it! And it's set that way cause you can't seem to get yourself ready for the school bus on time. Anyway, I know you've been pigging out on corn chips all afternoon, and don't tell me you haven't. Did you eat the whole bag?! Or maybe you ate two bags. I wouldn't put it past you." She scoffs for added effect, letting her eyes follow down his body just so he knows that she knows how fat he's become.

Crazy Louie now lets loose with more of his vulgar insults, which need no elaboration.

When she explains about talking with Marian and silencing her phone and the time getting away from her, he pivots abruptly and throws in several nasty spikes to the effect that maybe she, Dani, is so fat she doesn't need to eat anymore and doesn't care if others die of starvation right there on the kitchen floor.

"Get out!" shouts Dani, rushing him with a sauce pan with its handle pointed toward him, like a stampeding rhinoceros. Crazy Louie backs up, his legs nearly getting in his way, as she closes the kitchen door, shutting him out.

Truth is, after having Marian's bowl of soup and her chicken salad sandwich, she isn't nearly as hungry as she usually is at this time of day, although she too usually has snacks after school.

"What's for supper?" he asks through the door.

"Nothing. You said you've eaten."

He uses more expletives and bangs on the door, but Dani has put her foot against it. "Cabbage pie or pizza? Which do you want?" she says.

"I want pizza."

Smiling at her little joke of giving him a choice, Dani takes the pizza out of the freezer and turns on the oven. Then she turns her phone back on, seeing that Crazy Louie called her five times and left three texts, each expressing his advancing state of starvation. In his final message he'd said he was about to pass out.

She looks for a message from Cindy, too, but there is no message.

Dani proceeds to place the pizza on a pan and stick it in the oven. Then she makes room on the dining room table by pushing other things aside. She sets two places and two glasses with the silverware and napkins laid out. When this is done, she goes upstairs and takes a shower. Her mind keeps going over the things Marian said, and when she passes her tall mirror again, she removes her towel and stares at herself. Something inside her finds the image more abhorrent than it's ever been before. It reminds her of Cindy and her drawings, and she wonders if maybe it's come that time when Cindy is beginning to give up on her. Why was she ever friendly toward her in the first place when she has so many other friends?

Somehow, at age fifteen, at what should be the time her body begins to blossom like a flower and attract boys like so many bees, here she is totally fat and ugly and getting fatter and uglier by the minute! Pretty soon, she'll have skipped over all the fine years of beauty that every girl should enjoy and jumped right into the fat years for which even thin girls seem destined these days. It'll be like missing two or three whole decades. But this thought only reminds her that Marian is a lot older than fifty, and she's not even remotely fat. Dani somehow knows that Marian Natoli-Cantonia, who picked beans and peaches when she was twelve and won dancing contests in her teens and twenties, was never fat.

She takes the pizza out of the oven, opens the kitchen door again, and calls up the stairs.

"Hey, Crazy! It's ready!"

He comes clomping down the stairs. He sees the table is set nicely, but piles three slices of pizza on a plate, grabs a diet cola, and walks out, leaving Dani there to eat by herself. Of course, she is not surprised. Except for Sunday dinners and a few holidays, they've been eating in their rooms for years. She doesn't even know why she bothered to set the dining table like that. She never has. On the other hand, why would anybody want a sit-down meal using good china and silverware when it's only pizza? Yeah, right, *silverware*.

"Here," she says, stopping Crazy Louie before he's gone. She hands him the napkin, and he snaps it from her hand and goes on.

Nevertheless, she sits at the table and spreads a napkin on her lap. She pours her diet cola into a proper glass, places one slice of pizza on her plate, and begins cutting it with a knife and eating it with a fork, taking little sips and bites like she did with Marian's iced tea, soup, and sandwich.

One thing she needs to add to her list of groceries—candles.

17

The walking to Fletchers and the coming home with groceries, then the meeting of Marian and the talk and all the new ideas—it all seems to have filled her brain with exciting new thoughts and worn her out. After checking her phone again for signs of Cindy, Dani reclines on her bed feeling down. She's called Cindy once today.

You don't want to be a pest!

She looks at the ceiling now. This would be to gaze at the poster of Tom Selleck that's pinned there. She stares at him there, wondering what it might be like to have a boyfriend. Certainly it's nothing like having a teddy bear. After gazing long enough and thinking and imagining it, her eyes fold shut and she drifts off to sleep.

A few hours later it's the sound of her mother coming home and Crazy Louie's monotone starting up. Dani knows a rant when she hears one, even if the words are inaudible. The walls, floors, and ceilings vibrate with the tension of incriminating issuances that drone on and on. Dani goes to her music box that's in the top drawer of her dresser. She takes out one of her Enya CDs and places this in the player. Then she sits at her desk under a lamp and begins writing in her notebook. Maybe she can fill a page with Styrofoam peanuts by the time Crazy finishes his rant. She begins writing about bumping into another shopper's cart and carrying groceries in the Radio Flyer. She writes about the increased cost of soup, the endless varieties of everything, and how children used to pick peaches and help their parents make ends meet.

By the time she appears in the kitchen wearing her super-sized bathrobe over her jumbo pajamas, Crazy Louie and her mother are sitting there at the dinette table and it appears to Dani her mother's already suffered from his rant for so long her beer's gone flat.

Crazy Louie looks at Dani with bilious resentment, having now heard how things stand: his little sister is his new boss and likely to become keeper of the purse strings. He slides back his chair and gets to his feet, whispering the B word as he passes by her to leave the room. Her mother hears it but ignores it and watches him go out.

"I'll be up in a minute to tuck you in, sweetie," she says to him, but he does not answer. He bounds up the stairs and slams his door. Turning to Dani, she says, "Would you please, for God sakes, get me another beer, hon?" Dani does this and places it on the table there before her. "So I can't wait to hear about *your* day. Crazy Louie says you starved him to death, and you met some lady who says she's his great, great aunt. This should be good." Conni takes the beer up and takes a pretty good swallow. When Dani reaches for it, Conni draws it away. "You better not be drinking this when I'm not around."

"I wouldn't think of it." This is mostly true and Dani never has. "If I ever did, *he* would tell you."

Her mother laughs and says, "Yeah, he probably would," then pushes the beer toward her. Usually, Conni does not encourage her to sip from her beers, but the situation has obviously come to a head. Extreme conditions call for extreme measures, and everyone could use a bit of mellowing.

"Can't we find a foster home for him?" asks Dani. "Can't you put a listing in the newspaper? Something about offering a fine boy. Take him home today, along with his skateboard and bike, clothing included. He causes no trouble as long as you don't forget to feed him."

"Darling, your idea is tempting, believe me. But God help me, I need the tax deduction."

They laugh, and Dani sips the beer.

"Poor thing," says her mother. "He isn't a bad boy. Can't you be a *little* nicer to him?"

"Don't get me started on this topic, Mom."

"Alright then. Whatcha got for me?"

"I met a very nice lady today, and I'm going to Fletchers with her tomorrow morning. She's gunna advise me about my grocery list. Her name's Marian Natoli-Cantonia."

"I've heard the name before somewhere."

"She was a teller at National Bank, then a VP in public relations. Probably her name was in the newspaper a lot. She's our neighbor from down the street. But I need more money. I got nowhere near enough. Not even close." Dani does the thing with her fingers again, beckoning the cash to appear in a flash.

"How could you possibly need more money?!" Just short of anger, her mother's tone is abrupt.

"Cause I checked out the store and saw that they have a lot of specials. In order to get the best prices, I need to take advantage of the specials, which cost more up front but will save in the long run."

"What sort of specials?" her mother asks.

"All kinds of them. Usually the kind that trap you into buying two of something. Oh, but you wouldn't know about specials like that cause you only buy our groceries at the gas station."

"It's a handy mart."

"It's a gas station. That's why there's people getting gas and why there's hardly anything in the house. You only do little stop-offs for day-to-day. You don't plan ahead. Same way you buy gas—a gallon here and a gallon there. A few dollars here, a few dollars there. When was the last time you filled up your tank? You go around all the time on empty. If I'm to do any sort of serious cooking, I need to buy stuff and have stuff on hand for it. But it won't cost that much every week. It's just for right now. I have to buy a lot more stuff than usual, cause the tank's on *emmm-pteee*."

"Just where are you going to store all this *stuff*?"

"We have a pantry. I'm going to clean it out."

"And where will you put *that* stuff?"

"In the basement where it belongs."

"And where will you put all the stuff in the basement to make room for all the stuff in the pantry?"

"You needn't worry about it. I'm going to take care of everything."

"You get Louie to help you."

"It'll be easier if I just do it myself."

"I've got to work tomorrow night, so I won't be home for dinner. How much more do you need?"

"Could you spare a hundred?"

Her mother gasps, then stares at her a moment as if she'd grown horns from her head. You'd think she was asking for a big-screen TV for her bedroom.

"Are you gunna need CPR, Ma? Cause I'm not sure I know how to do that."

"Have you gotten into crack at that school of yours?! I'm hearing it's a big thing now. Lots of samplers are being handed out. They're advising us at the hospital to watch out for signs. Let me see your eyes."

"Mom! I'm serious! Sixty dollars isn't enough, and I've already spent some on the little bit I got today. I'm planning on actually cooking food— real food—you know, like with recipes where you need actual ingredients, like for pies and pancakes and cookies? I'd like to try baking some peach cobbler."

"Peach cobbler!" her mother laughs. "Where'd that come from? Peach cobbler!" she laughs with a snort.

"Oh, go ahead! Laugh all you want!"

"That's not real food, you know...peach cobbler!" She laughs it up and sips her beer.

"Mom! There's like nothing in this house to cook anything with—no *in-gred-i-ents*! *Nuh-thing!* Even our mice have left!"

"The mice have left cause they can't stand listening to your brother's rap music anymore, say nothing of getting any food here!"

"No. It's cause they're *star-ving*, Mom. Their babies are *dy-ing* cause their mothers can't breastfeed them anymore. Poor little babies."

"There's a good reason for it, you know." Her mother cups her hands as if to shout and says, "Earth to Dani! Earth to Dani! Helloo-oo . . . WE ARE BRO-OOKE!"

"How can you be broke? You just got paid."

"Well, I didn't wanna say anything, but I'm sorry for being a spoiler. I'm thinking ahead and wanna buy another car. It's for Crazy Louie for his graduation. But—shhhhh. It's for you to drive, too. For both of you."

"You're going to put CRA-ZEE LOU-IE behind the wheel of a car? Are you nuts?"

"Now, now. Don't be like that."

"I'm looking out for *his* safety and everybody else's," says Dani.

"These past few years haven't been easy for him. So give him a break."

"Oh, and it has been for me?"

"It's different for boys. Never mind. Your dad and I are discussing it."

"Well, how about we discuss money for food and you break into your little car fund? I'm your new cook. I'm your new organizer of the food pantry and your future house manager. I promise in the long run I will save you money." There's a pause and Dani adds, "Besides that, I'm taking over virtual responsibility for your crazy son. He'll have to come to me now. I'll be getting all the complaints cause all you'll have to say is go see Dani."

"You know, that's your best argument yet for all this. That's a good one. I'm gunna write it down. So, tell me, however did you meet this new aunt of yours? She gunna be your new advisor?"

"Don't start blaming *her* now. This has nothing to do with her."

"I didn't say that. I'm just curious. All of a sudden it's like money grows on trees with you."

"I met her today. I helped her carry her groceries home. She's offered to give me advice." After a pause, while her mother stares at her, Dani adds, "She's that woman in the red cape, who's always walking past our house. And you always say *people should do more walking like she does,* and when I want a ride downtown you always say *why don't you walk like Little Red Riding Hood does?*"

"That's her? A bank VP?"

"Retired."

"What sort of advice is Little Red Riding Hood going to give you?"

"Maybe the kind of advice you'd expect a grown-up Little Red Riding Hood to give. Maybe some advice about keeping the wolves away. Maybe some food advice. Her sister's a nutritionist. She works at the hospital."

"What's her name?"

"Teressa something."

"That's her sister?"

"Would she make it up? So Marian's offered to give me some tips. She seems to know a lot of stuff. She even thinks we could buy our own house."

"Oh, right! So she really is from a fairy tale!"

"Mom!" Dani holds out an empty palm, beckoning with her fingers. "Out with it."

"Fine. So we can expect hospital meals now."

"I thought you liked hospital food. You always say it's so yummy."

Objecting with only a *humph!*, Dani's mother goes for her purse on the counter and takes out three more twenties and hands these to her. "If you say it'll save us money, then it better save us money. That's part of the phone bill."

Dani wiggles her fingers some more. "I need a hundred, Mom. Mr. Crazy's car will have to wait."

Her mother purses her lips and takes out two more twenties. "I better see results." Shaking her finger, she adds, "God help you if I don't! I'll put *you* in a foster home!"

18

Saturday brings another sunny day and one that's even warmer. But when Dani sees that it's sunny outside, she looks at her alarm clock only to realize she's overslept. That's because she stayed awake till very late reading an article in her mother's glamour magazine about how to please a man in bed, curious to see if the suggestions in the article line up with the suggestions Cindy Rand has given her. It's eight-thirty already! She bolts from her bed, brushes her teeth and hair, puts on her fat sweats, then creeps down the stairs. The house is quiet. The kitchen smells like toasted bagels and there's hot water in the thermos, left there by her mother who's already gone to her morning job at Ozzy's Diner. There's instant oatmeal waiting for her on the table, but there's no time for breakfast. By now it's ten of nine and Dani puts on her shoes and jacket and goes out to the garage.

Just as she's pulling the wagon around in front of the house, she notices how drab their place looks with its weathered paint and the few scraggly shrubs. But the whole neighborhood looks the same. Most of the larger houses were converted to apartments a long time ago and now serve the often transient population of the community college, hospital, and nursing school—not exactly the kind of neighborhood where you'd expect the houses to be anything but drab and poorly maintained.

Yet Marian's house was not only well maintained but the grounds were neatly groomed and the shrubs well trimmed—forsythia trimmed into neat balls soon to be covered by tiny yellow buds. The tiny sprouting leaves of daffodils and tulips, planted within neatly arranged gardens, were proof of someone's keen attention to detail. Not to mention how Marian's lawns had been raked free of last year's leaves.

And how proud was Marian to show her the violet crocuses! In her whole life Dani's hardly given crocuses a moment's thought. But Marian, after walking all that ways, had taken a whole entire moment and gone out of her way to admire them and to show Dani how beautiful and fragile they were and to explain how they come before all the other flowers and bloom quickly and are just as quickly gone.

"Just think of it! Their brief little blossoms just popping up from the cold hard ground like that—because somebody wanted to bring a little joy into the world. You know, a lotta times the people who planted them are no longer with us. It seems so sad. Yet I feel so happy when I see them."

Dani now takes herself to the edge of her house, back a ways from the street, to where something's caught her eye. And what do you know? There amid the old dead leaves is a little patch of yellow and violet—her very own crocuses, their ironic petals poking up through a layer of leaves and dirt to catch the sunlight. She bends closer to get a better look at them, clearing the leaves away and noticing for the first time in her life the incredible design of this tiny flower, remembering what Marian said yesterday about there being *no detail too insignificant for God's attention.* Dani draws out her iPhone to photograph them.

From behind her comes a voice. "Well, you seem to have found a few little friends."

"Good morning!" says Dani, turning to see Marian wearing her cape's hood drawn over her head against the chilly air.

"And what a fine morning it is!" says Marian. "And what a fine little sign of spring you have there!"

"Hey, look at this." Dani steps over to show her the photos.

"Oh, my word! Would you look at that!" Marian holds the phone up closer. "You know, you've just given me a good reason to get me one of these gadgets."

"You don't have a phone?"

"Oh, I have a phone, alright! Don't tell me about it. But would you look at this? Do you know, Dani, each little thing there has a name? These yellow things sticking up are the anthers. That thing in the middle is the stigma. Down lower on the stigma is the ovary, and all of them together, they're called the pistil."

"I'd be willing to show you how the phone works sometime," says Dani. "Then you'll want one of your own."

"At the moment, it's tempting. But I do just fine without it. Besides, I hear from my son all the time about how expensive they are. And I hear there's a few places around here where they don't even work. Thanks, but I do love the photos."

The two set off for Fletcher's Market.

"My mother gave me a hundred dollars more," says Dani.

"If you buy all those things on your list, I'm afraid you'll need every penny and then some."

"Yeah, but I didn't dare ask for more."

After a moment, Marian says, "When I was a girl, a hundred and sixty dollars was more than most people made in two or three weeks. And it had to cover everything. We could have bought two months' worth of food with a hundred and sixty dollars. But, of course, we didn't have all these fancy different kinds of food and instant things. My mother bought our food more in bulk form. She made her own things. She baked all our bread. She made her own tomato sauce. She had a big garden and she canned everything. And we helped. We had peaches and pears all winter. She made her own pickles. We had a fruit cellar with bushels of potatoes in it, and my little sisters and I had to pick off the sprouts. Have you ever had to pick off potato sprouts?"

"I don't even know what potato sprouts are?"

"They're the first little roots of the potatoes as they begin to grow into new plants. That happens in the winter, and you have to keep the sprouts off or the potato will get all mushy. Potatoes are best kept in a cool and dark place."

"I don't buy potatoes," says Dani.

"But you have them on your list."

"That's instant potatoes."

"Oh, heavens sakes!" Marian gives her a stern look.

"What?!"

"Never mind. You have much worse things than instant potatoes on your list." Marian scoffs sternly, but she's smiling nevertheless, walking along there.

"For example?"

"You know, we really ought to sit down over a cup of coffee and talk about your list. I need to explain some things to you."

"Like what kind of things?" Dani is pulling the empty wagon that's going clack-clack, clack-clack on the sidewalk, and they're walking, and Marian is once again stepping along like one of those speed walkers she's seen at the park, their arms swinging in a great show. Dani has to step along too, and there's soreness in her legs from yesterday's walk—a very fat sort of soreness!

Clack-clack, clack-clack…

Marian looks sideways at her and says, "Dani, have you had a good breakfast yet?"

"I skipped breakfast. I got up a bit too late. I usually stay up till Mom comes home from the hospital, and we talk for a while. Otherwise, I don't get to see her all that much. Also, I started writing my Home Ec paper last night. And then I was reading an article on sex in a glamor magazine cause I couldn't sleep cause all the grocery shopping and everything tired me out so bad I took a nap after supper."

"What did the glamor magazine say about sex?"

"How to please a man in bed." Dani giggles, covering her mouth with her fingers. "But I doubt I'll ever need the tips."

"Good. I hope you don't need them for a long, *long* time."

Dani giggles, privately hoping the opposite.

"And what do you usually eat for breakfast?" asks Marian.

"It's like oatmeal and a bagel."

"That's it?"

"No, that's not all. It's a raisin bagel with cream cheese. And the oatmeal usually has, like, apples or bananas in it, and can we walk any faster? I'm about to be run over by this speeding wagon!"

Marian laughs out loud and slows her gate. "I'm sorry. You poor thing! And you're awfully funny. I really like you, you're so funny!"

They both take a slower gait now, and the wagon calms down its clacking on the upheaved sidewalk blocks, the noise sounding more like the soft clicking of the trains that run along River Street that Dani's heard many times.

"Since you buy instant spuds," says Marian, going on with it, "I expect this oatmeal is instant, too?"

"Is there any other kind?" Dani grins and adds, "It's a lot faster, you know. There's like only five minutes to get ready for school in the morning."

"It's also loaded with sugar," adds Marian.

"Are you kidding? I have to *add* sugar?"

"I can't imagine it, needing more! What about Louis?"

"He usually eats cereal. He likes honey oats or Frosted Flakes. But he likes bagels and cream cheese, too."

"In your new job as house manager, do you plan to fix breakfasts for everyone?"

"Well, I hadn't thought about it. But yes, I suppose if I'm to be the cook, that should include breakfast."

"Well, we certainly have a lot to talk about. What do you say we stop in at Carina's and have us a breakfast, and take a moment to discuss your list?"

For a fraction of a second, Dani hesitates.

"It's my treat," says Marian.

19

Carina's Diner is on Main Street, and to get there, Marian and Dani cross Church Boulevard and walk up Elm and take a right onto Main. The downtown diner is on the corner of Main and Central Avenue, just up the street from Fletcher's Market. Dani parks the wagon near the door.

"You better bring that inside if you don't have a lock for it."

"You really think some kid'll steal it?"

Marian's eyes flash to several adult homeless people with shopping carts who typically gather out front of the diner, where those with enough money come in to get a cup of soup or coffee, and those without money stand on the corner asking for handouts, often holding cardboard signs saying things like "HUNGRY AND OUT OF WORK" or "GOD BLESS YOU!"

"You better bring it in where you can keep an eye on it."

Marian holds the door open as Dani pulls the wagon in, and they go in and Marian chooses a table with four chairs off to the side in a corner where it's quiet, and they take off their coats, draping them over two chairs. They sit at right angles, both more or less facing the door. When the waitress comes, Marian orders a cup of coffee, a small glass of grapefruit juice, two eggs, and two slices of bacon, adding, "Please hold the potatoes and toast."

When the waitress turns to Dani, embarrassment flushes her face. Dani doesn't eat out much. Actually, never. It's all quite a novel thing to do. She hesitates, then says, "I'll have the same."

"Should I also hold the potatoes and toast?" asks the waitress. *Considering how fat you are*, she does not say.

"Yes," says Dani, "hold the potatoes and toast."

Although her mouth is watering and her hunger is palpable—now that real food is nigh. Something like an intuition tells her Marian is not keen on hash brown potatoes and toast and this may be a time to show restraint.

Marian turns to her and says, "Dani, why don't we split them?" To the waitress: "She'll take the potatoes and toast. Be sure to make the potatoes extra crispy."

"White, whole wheat, or rye?" asks the waitress.

"Whole wheat's fine," says Dani.

When the waitress leaves, Dani says, "You're awfully tactful."

"I think that waitress was awfully rude."

"I can't blame her. I think it's true that fat people *look* hungry." Dani covers her chuckle.

Marian laughs, too. "Stop it!"

"It's true. And in this case especially! Cause I'm starved! But I was trying to go light on your pocketbook."

"You're a darling. But the price is the same either way."

When the coffee is served, along with the creamer and sweetener, Dani takes up a bag of the artificial sweetener and pours it into her cup. She pours in the creamer and stirs it, and when she sips it, she pours in another bag of the artificial sweetener, stirring it well. This tastes better, and she notices Marian staring at her with eyes so freaked out it's like she's seen a green Martian.

"What?!" she says, breaking out with a giggle.

"*You* is what! God help me, how much of that sweetener you eat!" Marian holds up a bag of it, wagging it back and forth. "This is your *sugar*?"

"It's better than sugar!" Dani laughs. "There's like zero calories."

"Look at me here!" Marian, using a firm tone, points her two fingers at her own two eyes like bad guys do in movies. Dani focuses and tries to stifle another giggle. "No, it is NOT better!"

"Well, that's what everybody says."

"Is that so? Well, then please explain to me why everyone is so fat these days, if this stuff is *better?!*" She takes the bag and tosses it back into the sugar bowl like it's a freaking worm. Then she takes out a bag of actual sugar. "See here? This is poison, too." She takes up the brown bag now. "This is your least harmful poison—unrefined, organic sugar. The white sugar is heavily processed using synthetic chemicals to remove the impurities to make it white. The artificial sweetener is a chemical. So your first dietary lesson of the day is to avoid chemicals by any means; avoid processed foods whenever you can; and use as little natural cane sugar as possible, preferably none!"

"So every kind of sweetener is bad for you?" asks Dani, giggling stupidly.

"All sugar is bad for you. But to distinguish between white and the so-called natural sugars, I have a simple rule. It's a rule I use for everything, whether it's food or cosmetics—avoid anything that's processed using chemicals or that contains chemicals. Dani—you must listen to me here. Listen. Why are so many people getting cancer these days? Parkinson's disease? Alzheimer's disease? A hundred others?"

"Cause they're sick," says Dani.

"Oh, you precious thing cause they're sick!"

"Well, I don't know."

"Well, I can tell you this: it most likely is not *cause* they're living in a clean and chemical-free environment or *cause* they're eating clean and chemical-free foods!"

Dani can't stop herself from giggling at Marian, cause Marian's so like having a freaking fit.

"You like that word *cause*, eh?"

Marian purses her lips at her. "You're too sweet for your own good."

"But it doesn't actually do me any good," says Dani, flatly.

There is a pause when Marian just stares at her, then says, "If you want to get yourself out of this fix you're in, you better get serious!" Marian's voice is scolding.

Dani straightens up like a little boy being told to straighten up in church. But she's still fighting the giggle impulse. "I'm very serious. I promise. I'm listening. And I *will* follow your advice."

"Will you *really*?"

"Yes. I will. That's a promise! I will follow every word of your advice even if it kills me!" She giggles.

"I'm going to hold you down and sit on you!"

"You know, there are a few boys who are afraid of me."

"I will do it!"

Dani is laughing and can't help it. "Alright, but you won't have to. I promise. Double promise!"

"Alright then. We'll just see if you will. *Cause*...if you don't, you know where you're headed? Do I have to tell you where you're headed?"

"No. I know where I'm headed. I like totally get it. My mother's glamour magazines have other articles besides on sex, and most of those are on the topic of what happens eventually to fat people."

"So, let us continue then. Your number one priority, to help avoid all sorts of diseases and stay healthy, is to avoid chemicals."

"I'm afraid I wouldn't know where to begin with that," says Dani. "Just being honest. Not to argue or anything. But aren't chemicals, like, in *every-thing*?—even the air we breathe?"

"I know. It's about impossible. And not everyone would agree with me on this about sugar. Not even nutritionists agree. But I tend to take a circumspect view of things. All my life I've seen new things come out and there's somebody saying it's perfectly healthy, but sometime later they discover the thing causes cancer. You've heard a hundred stories like that I'm sure. It seems to happen all the time. One minute they say sunscreen is an absolute must; another time they're saying you should avoid it and just cover up and avoid the sun. And that's all about chemicals in the sunscreen, and a lot of other skin products. Don't humans just make the best guinea pigs!"

While that settles into Dani's head, Marian takes out the notebook paper of the shopping list and unfolds it. "Dani, I hardly know where to begin with your grocery list. Especially when I see you have listed *sugar*, when I know what you really mean is a chemical poison."

"Can I just ask a question?" says Dani. "If artificial sweeteners are poisons, how come they allow them in our foods?"

"The honest answer is it's *me* saying this. Me. *I'm* saying they're poisons. I've read a lot of things. I've read the good, the bad, and the ugly. You can get all this on line. You can do your own reading on line or in a hundred books. There's probably something about this in your magazines. Like I said, my view is circumspect. These things I'm going to tell you are my own views based on years of reading. You can also find lots of YouTube videos on lots of topics. I've processed a lot of information and have come to certain general conclusions that always trend toward the side of caution. So I've come to have my own views. This is all about whether or not you're willing to take my advice."

"Well, you don't come across as *UN*healthy. So that says something. So just start at the top."

"There's really no top." Marian chuckles at this absurdity.

"Yes, there is," says Dani. "See?" She reaches over and points to the first item on the list—"cola."

"Alright, there's a top. But what I mean is there's a whole world of understanding food that a person *should have* before they can begin to make up a proper and healthy grocery list."

"Well, you said I should be objective, so objective I'll be."

"What I mean is, very few of us are trained nutritionists. Maybe I have learned a few things from my sister, who *is* a nutritionist, but what I really have is my gut sense of things. Like I just said—having a circumspect view and basing decisions on my own private and very limited knowledge, which is mostly taking this and that piece of information and forming my own unique food policy."

"Alright, I understand," says Dani. "You're not an expert. It's only your own opinion. But you sound like you know a few things. And like I say, you don't look like you've been following an *UN*healthy diet. So alright. I'm listening. And I've decided to heed your advice."

"Well, take for example your cola." Marian once more takes up the bag of artificial sweetener. "Now I know you don't mean regular cola. What you mean is *diet cola*—this." She now wags the packet of artificial sweetener before Dani's eyes. "Do I need to say more?"

"I guess not."

"But I do need to, because it's a big topic. While there's a lot of information about the dangers of these artificial sweeteners, there's been just as many articles written by researchers about the harms of sugar itself. So, either one you choose, if you have a serious sweet tooth, which you seriously have, you'll be causing chaos in your body."

"You think I have a sweet tooth?"

Marian smiles and touches Dani's cheek with her fingers. "You're so sweet, how could you not have a sweet tooth?" Then she pinches the fat of her jowl.

Dani laughs at Marian's kidding around, but knows in her bones she's addicted to sweet things. Besides that, her mother's always telling her so.

"Your next item is bagels, then bread, then corn chips," says Marian. "Generally, I have an issue with instant potatoes or instant anything, but only on the basis of its actual ingredients, if you consider the list of them. Another thing, as you already know, is your instant oatmeal. That's loaded with sugar. But it also has other ingredients besides oatmeal. In the first place, we've already discussed processed foods and why you should avoid them. Sometimes try looking on the labels to see what's in a product. When you see a long list of words you can't pronounce, that's a hint of trouble. Since you're not a scientist, it's probably a good bet your body won't like words you can't pronounce. But you've got your handy phone. Why not put it to use? Look a few things up and inform yourself about these chemicals. I know there are websites that talk about the harms of food additives. If you add this information to your Home Ec paper you'll surely get an A. Another thing my sister taught me—avoid products with food flavoring. If it has *flavoring* of any kind, that's more chemicals which won't be listed on the label."

Dani grins and says, "Uh oh. Just thought of something."

"What?"

"My oatmeal is also sugar-free!"

They both laugh together at the hilarity of this. Marian shakes her head in frustration. "You're a walking chemical processor! Have I said enough on this topic?"

"Alright, I get it," says Dani. "You need not say more on the topic of sugar and chemicals. And I have an inkling my entire list needs revising."

"Yeah, it sorta does." Laughing again, Marian says, "I'm sorry. I don't mean to make light of it. It's a very serious topic we're discussing, and it has a major impact on your life and your goals. In your case, it will have an impact on your brother Louis, too. If you prepare meals for your mom, then she's in the loop as well. In fact, *this* (Marian holds the note paper up and gives it a little shake). This will have a profound effect on everyone you ever prepare meals for—your family, your future husband, and your future children." The words sink in for a second, and Marian adds, "This piece of paper represents the greatest obstacle standing between you and good health and the achievement of your goals in life, and please notice I'm not laughing."

The words are stunning, and Dani doesn't know what to say.

20

he waitress comes with the plates of food and sets them on the table, bringing in her apron a bottle of ketchup. Dani looks at her plate and feels her stomach growling in veracious hunger. Maybe there are two cats in there fighting it out. Marian thanks the waitress, and while Dani takes her napkin and places it on her lap she notices Marian bow her head in silent grace. Dani politely waits a moment before taking up the ketchup and squirting a handsome quantity over her hash browns.

"Are you religious?" she asks Marian.

"I wouldn't call it that. Perhaps a better word is *humble in the presence of God*. I also feel inclined to thank the Lord for my food, but not to make too much of a show of it. Paul in the Bible, you know, said not to. Publicly, I mean."

"Were you ever hungry?" asks Dani.

"Although I myself have never lived through times when food was scarce, my parents surely did, and my mother was keen to always remind me what it was like during the Great Depression when so many were without work, and I learned from those stories that during hard times, having food on the table in any kind of abundance was not possible for most people. My mother used to say, when she was growing up, her mother added water to the stew."

After taking a bite or two from her plate, Marian says, "You know, I was very fortunate to be born only a few years after World War II ended—1951. My dad had joined the Army after arriving in America, so my memories are of him begin when he brought home some pieces of lumber and began to make a rocking horse. I watched him make it, cutting all the pieces on a jigsaw, then using chisels and files to shape and smooth them by hand, making little hooves and quite a dainty-looking face. When he put it all together, it really looked like a horse. When he painted it he gave it these big brown eyes and long eyelashes. He painted the lips red, and not just a calm and warm red, but a brilliant China red like my cape, a red that shouts boldly with joy. He carefully trimmed the wood so there were these two ears that looked like the wind was blowing them backward, as if the horse were running in a race. While he was doing that, he made a rifle out of a scrap of wood. It was quite a nice-looking rifle, too. My brother Joey, two years younger than I was—he kept that rifle beside his bed and carried it like a soldier on a sling made of clothesline, and my father—I remember how he used to tell him how important it was because our nation would not be free or even a very safe place without guns, and every responsible boy and man should have one. Of course, I too played with that rifle. Joey and I exchanged my playing with his rifle for his riding on my horse. But he always preferred to carry the rifle with him when he rode the horse. He also wore a cowboy hat and carried shiny pistols at his hips. You know, it's ironic, but we learned most all we knew about cowboys and cowgirls and a whole world of moral values from listening to the Lone Ranger on the radio."

"My mother would have a heart attack if Louis ever got hold of a toy gun," says Dani. "Much less a real one."

"Louis is how old?"

"He's seventeen."

"Then he's plenty old enough to have his own real gun and to hunt. Your dad ought to teach him about guns, and he should take a gun safety course."

Dani says with eyes rolling, "I wouldn't trust him with a slingshot."

"Tss, tss, tss," says Marian. "What have we done to our young men? What will become of them?"

"It's just the way the world is now," says Dani. "Boys aren't really supposed to be boys anymore. It seems they want girls to be boys and boys to be girls. Maybe in the middle there's something we don't yet have a name for. Maybe they'll be called *genderless human entities*."

Marian laughs. "I know the name of it. It's called *socially engineered chaos*. Like those homeless people out there. Asking for handouts no less! When Tommy can't find anyone to do simple work like lawn mowing, painting, and cleaning! Imagine it! Right outside that door! *Out of work?!* His sign ought to say *I refuse to work!* Do you know, Dani, the orchards have to hire immigrants to pick their fruit because the local born-free Americans won't work!

"But, of course, nowadays," continues Marian, "people have all but forgotten how the real and proper God-made world is supposed to work, or *Nature-made* if you prefer. There actually are laws about these things, you know. Nature makes them. And she doesn't like it when her laws are broken. If you ignore natural laws, what you get is chaos. Which worries me quite a bit. Society's arrogance! Thinking you can play around with the fundamental laws of Nature and of God and expect a good outcome."

Dani looks out the large window of Corina's, watching the pedestrians on the sidewalk giving money to the poor people there.

"They do the same with economics," adds Marian after taking a sip of her coffee. "There's laws to that, too. Another thing that amazes me is how people so easily forget history. You forget the mistakes of history, and history will surely repeat itself. President Harry Truman said, *The only thing that's new is the history you don't know.* But it seems all our institutions today are run by people who've completely forgotten history."

Dani smiles at this old quote, but keeps working on her eggs, bacon, and hash brown potatoes. She's worked up a way to place an egg between two slices of the toast and to eat it like a sandwich, while Marian nibbles at her eggs and bacon and sips her coffee slowly and rambles on with old-folk talk.

"But you know," continues Marian, "I think Harry Truman was only referring to historic events and realities of survival. Because there really are new things that we didn't know before. I find this so ironic. For example, we've learned amazing things about food—nutrition. And we know the harm so many processed foods have done to our health, and also to our brains, by the overconsumption of sugar, gluten, and by the use of chemicals in nearly all our foods.

"But I find it so ironic that we've raised several generations of children on poor diets, starting with junk food in the fifties and gradually expanding the junk menu until it's overtaken and replaced wholesome foods in grocery stores. Used to be when you ate junk you knew it was junk. But today, you can eat junk and the label on the package actually says it's healthy. We've just about completely ruined children's diets with sugar, artificial flavoring, and sweeteners—fast foods and massive amounts of candy. Not to mention all the bad fats we've been eating our whole lives because somebody said it was healthier to replace real butter made from real cream with vegetable fat."

"Wait a minute. Are you saying butter is better?"

"If it's made with real cow's cream I am absolutely saying that. Again, you can use your phone to read about it, but be careful because there's still a lot of bad science associated with this topic. Go to westonaprice.org. You can learn a lot there."

"I just assume that if it's something put out by scientists, it must be true," says Dani.

"Sorry, but many scientists tend to say what their bosses want them to say. But this about the food is only one thing. While we've been increasing the junk food, at the same time we've gradually turned our children into couch potatoes, where they can't possibly burn off all those calories and fat.

"As if that's not bad enough," adds Marian, "we seem unable or unwilling to make the connection between poor diet and children—especially boys—that are so keyed up and so hyperactive that we feel the need to further contaminate their brains with chemical drugs. Then we add insult to them by feeding their minds with images of the most violent sort. How could anyone think this is a good way to raise children?"

"You're talking about the internet," says Dani.

"And video games."

"You should see the kinds of video games Crazy Louie spends hours a day playing in his room," says Dani. "You know what I think? I truly think sometimes Crazy Louie is a real living zombie."

"And when these zombies turn around and shoot up a school," says Marian, "we blame it all on the guns!"

Suddenly Marian looks up at Dani and says, "Oh, listen to me! This is not at all what I intended to talk about! And you really need to stop calling him Crazy!" For the first time, Dani detects a bit of a crust on Marian's voice.

"I will work on that. I promise."

"Here's something from my success seminar. Remember this: *thoughts are things*. Words have the power to pollute your mind and produce negative energy. They also have the power to effect positive results. Be careful what you think and say. Try always to be positive. And I guess in our new world of videos, the same is true for images you allow into your mind. It's important to protect the mind, especially the minds of our youth."

"That sounds otherworldly," says Dani. "That mere thoughts can become real things."

"It's true. You can think your way to success by controlling your thoughts. Flush out the negatives and invite the positives. The same is true when you think about and speak to others. Your words and thoughts cannot only cause other people harm, but they can cause you great harm, too."

"What? How?"

"Never mind. Just take my word for it—*thoughts are things*. Remember it. Now, tell me, does Louis have any kind of job?"

"No. Nor, I think, does he want one. He's been getting all his money from my mom and dad. I think my father feels guilty for having an affair and causing Mom and us to leave. And my mother feels guilty for not being home and for not keeping her husband happy."

"So, as a way of compensating, they give you money."

"It sounds a bit psycho-analytical but it's true," says Dani. "Mostly it's been Dad giving it. I mean, not always in the form of money, but it's more in the form of clothing, Louie's expensive video games, ski stuff and season passes. Stuff like that. My mother would be even more generous if she had more money to give us. To compensate, she lets Louie get away with all sorts of stuff, including disrespecting her. She just told me she's saving money to give him a car. I can hardly believe it."

Ignoring this, Marian asks, "You ski at Sky Mountain?"

"We always join the Ski Club at school. But Louie doesn't ski. He snowboards with his skateboard friends and continues to uphold his nickname."

"Well, that's a good sport, I think. I never skied. I wanted to, but could never afford it."

"Well, as it turns out, Louie and I will soon be like you. My dad's in over his head with medical bills and there's no money for skiing or even new clothes."

Marian looks at Dani a moment and considers what she's just said. "That reminds me, Dani. I've been thinking a lot about you and Louis since I met you—your situation and so forth. The summer's coming up. My son Tommy, he's always telling me how much trouble it is to find helpers to do different things. He and his son Flavio work together, but they're needing extra help this summer. I want some painting done on my houses and I'm bracing for the possibility that I'm going to lose a few tenants over the IsenellaFiber fiasco. If the company closes, I'll have a few vacancies. And a vacancy for me always represents an opportunity. I like to remodel when possible, but at least repaint. So I've got a feeling there's gunna be a lot of work coming up. And there's other things like mowing and trimming hedges and trees and so forth. Tommy has several exterior painting jobs, too. There's all sorts of things, really. Do you think you might want to earn some extra money?"

"I sure would."

"Maybe we should set a time I could stop in and we could all have a visit. I'd like your mom to be there, too. If you started working for Tommy, do you think you could bring Louie in and would you be willing to work with him? You'd be real good at encouraging him, if you know what I mean. Boys Louie's age, you know, they need more opportunities."

"Well, I'd be willing to try. But he needs a lot of inspiration."

"Most boys do."

"How about when we get back from Fletcher's you have lunch with me?" says Dani. "Mom won't be there, but I'll get Louie to join us."

21

ani and Marian are sitting at the little table at Corina's Diner, both having stretched the breakfast to an hour and refilled their coffees. Both plates are empty and pushed to the side. Dani feels stuffed. Then Marian says, "So, as for your grocery list, I guess we didn't finish with that topic very well, did we?"

"I'll have quite a time processing all the things you've told me," says Dani. "I have a feeling a lot of things on my list are bad and I'll have to re-think everything."

"I had to deal with that myself," says Marian. "It's the kind of thing people who want to believe what they hear from official sources have trouble disbelieving. I was no different. But I was older when I came to realize this. I was in my teens and twenties during the Vietnam era. I think a lot of people who lived through the Vietnam era don't have as much credulity in believing what we're told. We're told that wars are just but aren't, foods that we're told are safe but aren't; and some we're told aren't safe but are. Some people think obesity stems from genetics. There's even a push to normalize it. Do you know that catalogues are hiring obese models? The normalization of disease! It's a tragedy. But the disease is a mutual disease—the government having the disease of chronic dishonesty and the public beset by chronic gullibility. Lying then becomes the norm and thinking for oneself becomes a bridge too far."

"As it turns out," says Dani, "my family's got quite a history of disbelieving the government. I'm talking about my Native American family and their story of war with the government over Harmony Mountain."

"What was it all about?"

"The Federal Government hired a research corporation from Germany to trick the Northeast Tribal Council into leasing them some land. The idea was to investigate the healing effects of Harmony Mountain. Why does it sing? How do the healing springs heal? What are the healing properties of all the quartz crystals found all throughout the mountain? There were all these reports of people with various diseases being healed in the springs and caverns and sometimes by merely being on the mountain. And this German doctor began to do research for the Federal Government. Eventually, the owners of the mountain—that's basically my Grandma Anita's tribespeople—found the researchers were putting up fences to block us off our own land. Do you know, their intent was to take that mountain away from the Indians and also away from the public? It's true. They were selling favors to the rich—to politicians and VIP's."

"What sort of favors?" asks Marian.

"Inviting them to come and be healed. Like the mountain was some kind of fountain of youth reserved only for the special people. That's when the Tribal Council found it wasn't the researchers from Germany doing this, it was the Federal Government of the USA using them in a kind of proxy war trying to take over Harmony Mountain. It was the Federal Government that wanted that mountain. It came almost near a shooting war and my grandma and grandpa were right in the middle of it."

"You know what?" says Marian. "Having this experience in your own family puts you at a great advantage in life."

"How so?"

"I think you have a head start at overcoming one of your greatest challenges."

"What challenge is that?"

"That it's easier to deceive a man than it is to convince him he's been deceived."

"I think I'm beginning to see your point."

"I hope so," says Marian. "You're going to be severely challenged as we go further in our discussions." Gesturing toward the note paper in her hand, she adds, "I'm afraid this topic is going to turn you all around and inside out."

"I think I'm ready to be turned around."

"Okay…well…so here's the thing." Marian Natoli-Cantonia leans forward and crosses her arms on the table at Corina's Diner. "I seem to have realized a bit of insight just now as we've been talking. It was when you poured those bags of artificial sweetener into your coffee like that. Suddenly a light came on in my head and my memory was jarred loose. It came to me that it's taken me my whole life up to now to feel that I have any kind of intelligent understanding of food, imperfect as that may be. A lot of credit for any knowledge I have goes to my own inquisitive nature, with a lot of help from my younger sister, Teressa. And I must say, thinking about this, it comes to my mind that even her knowledge about food has been progressing slowly. Just the other day, she says to me, *You know, the knowledge I have now is remarkably more sophisticated than the things I was taught in college, and many of the things I was taught in college are wrong today.*

"My point is," continues Marian, "learning about food and nutrition is a work in progress. It can't be handed to a fifteen-year-old girl over break-fast as she's on her way to the store with a grocery list full of things no human who wants to be healthy should ever eat."

These are shocking words. But soon as Marian speaks them, questions pop into Dani's mind, and she asks, "What sort of world is it? What sort of government would allow a statement like that to be true?"

Marian smiles and adds, "I guess you're old enough to face a few facts of life. And one of them is disillusionment. Most people experience it at some point along the way. For me, it was the Kennedy assassination. Then Martin Luther King. Then Robert Kennedy. After three solid hits, I began to question things. Finally (and thankfully!), once and for all, I began to have doubts."

"I've started to question things, too," says Dani. "I can't figure out why our country, I mean our government, allows gangs and drugs in our schools. Did you know you can go right over to Stacy Ann Hastings Memorial Park and buy drugs? It isn't even close to being a secret."

There is a moment when neither speaks, like maybe they both have to reconcile the reality of life as it really is in Languishire in 2018.

22

moment passes before Marian continues with the discussion about food.

"Just so you know, all these things I'm saying about food come from my own opinion based on many years of traveling down my own learning path. Believe it or not, there was a time when I began to gain weight. Fortunately, I had the luxury of my sister's knowledge and support, mixed with just the right amount of incredulity that inspired me to go ahead and find a few answers all on my own. With my sister's help, I was able to come up with my own emergency plan for getting myself into a healthier way of eating and living."

Marian pauses and thinks. Then proceeds. "Listen carefully to what I'm about to say. Whatever knowledge I have is merely an interpretation of my own discoveries as I have pieced them together to form a way to understand my own biome and how it processes all the stuff I put in it. Everyone's a little different, you know. You can tell a lot about how your body is processing what you put in it by looking in the mirror and paying close attention to how your food makes you feel. For sure, you shouldn't be getting fat. You shouldn't be getting hungry only a few hours after eating."

Dani laughs out loud. "I don't even recall a time when I could get through the evening without eating a big snack before bedtime."

"That's often caused by your body wanting more sugar."

"But here's a question. I'm sure artificial sweeteners aren't good for me, but you said sugar is bad, too. I seem to be confused about sugar?"

"It's because your body is also confused. You've probably got some issues with glucose and insulin, an early sign of diabetes."

"What should I do?"

"First, I suggest you eat no actual sugar, none at all."

"Not even in coffee?"

"None. Zero. Try it black or with cream only. It'll taste awfully flat at first. But after a while you'll begin to notice even your cream or milk has a touch of sugar in it. Did you know cow's milk is really quite sweet when it's fresh-squeezed?"

"I used to be a farm girl, you know."

"Is that so?"

"A visiting one, but when I visited my grandfolks' farm, I was really a farm girl through and through. We drank fresh-squeezed milk, fresh eggs, and plenty of bacon. And I was thin in those days, come to think of it."

"We used to get our milk and eggs from a neighbor," says Marian. "And lots of people used to drink plenty of milk and eat plenty of bacon, and most all the people I ever knew growing up were not fat."

"But I like a little sugar in my coffee," says Dani.

"For now, try going without sugar or anything sweetened. No sweetened drinks. And absolutely nothing artificially sweetened. Pretty soon your taste buds will adjust and become more sensitive to sugar, and you'll see after a while how the flavor of things will come out more. After you give your taste buds a rest, you'll see that a tiny pinch of sugar or honey or even half a teaspoon of maple syrup in your coffee will be plenty.

"Another thing, I noticed in your refrigerator you do have milk. But I would reduce the amount of milk you drink. You might have a bit of lactose intolerance, and you may even have early symptoms of thyroid issues. It's more common in women and especially women who are overweight. So I suggest replacing cow's milk with coconut milk. But if you're going to drink milk, I suggest whole milk. This low-fat, no-fat fad is—well, it's a fad, used I think mostly to sell you an alternative that may be worse than the original. Your body needs fat. Don't forget that. I'll say it again, your body, especially your brain, needs fat. That's because your brain is made of fat."

"What else?"

"Nor should you be eating all the wheat products you're eating: the bread, the bagels, and all the pasta dishes you're planning to prepare according to your list here. There's gluten in those products, and gluten is a problem. For many people it causes serious disease—autoimmune disorder, thyroid disorder, diabetes—not to mention how it converts to sugar and then to fat stored in the gut. But gluten is tricky because it may be causing serious health issues that you don't notice. Take you, for example. You obviously eat a lot of it, yet you don't seem to have any actual allergies relating to it. Yet it is harming you, and I'd say it's responsible for most of the fat on your tummy. Belly fat is an early sign of diabetes, which is insulin resistance. Your blood has too much sugar in it, and the only thing your body knows to do is to store it as fat.

"While insulin is supposed to remove glucose from the blood and store it as fat, sometimes gluten finds its way directly into your blood through what they call a permeable gut, or leaky gut. When this happens, your body begins producing enzymes that attach themselves to glucose mole-cules the same way as insulin is supposed to attach itself. But if the enzymes are there, the insulin is denied access. This, in turn, prevents the insulin from taking the glucose or sugar out of your system. Your pancreas keeps getting a signal to make more and more insulin, and pretty soon your pancreas wears out and stops producing it. That's when you begin to have seriously high sugar in your blood, and that turns into diabetes.

"Another thing," Marian continues. "Snacks—all these potato chips and corn chips and cookies and crackers—for heaven's sakes! All of it is quite possibly killing you, and you don't even know it. But that's my point that I started to make. How do I pass on to you the understandings you need just to begin your journey out of this—I don't know what to call it."

"Call it the pits," says Dani. "I really think I'm in the pits. And so are a lot of the kids at school."

"Well, I'll say one thing. You seem to be ahead of the curve here. I mean, at your age. Most girls don't even begin to realize they're in the pits until it's too late. I mean, for all intent and purpose, too late for them to make any meaningful transition from a life of daily food poisoning to a reasonably healthy diet. For most people, once they become obese, they are so many years into poisoning themselves there's little hope for reversing the damage. I mean, there is a way, of course. There's always a way to lose weight and get healthier at any age. But for them to take that path? For them to take such a drastic turn after years and years of bad habits using poison food as comfort food…I don't think that's possible."

"It sounds so depressing."

"But you're only fifteen. I think you can get out of this. But it won't be possible for you, either, unless you yourself decide to make it so. It has to be your decision, your choice. It has to come from within you. Same for your brother. He has to want it, too. It's like his newspaper delivery job. He didn't want it badly enough. If he doesn't want this he'll fight you all the way. He'll want foods in the house that you can't eat. He'll want that diet cola, his chips, and all the other things. Healthy eating and living a healthy lifestyle is a very high summit to ascend to if you're all alone and climbing up from the valley without anyone to encourage and support you. Speaking of mountains, this is a big one and mostly you'll be climbing it alone."

"Am I totally in the valley?" asks Dani.

"This grocery list here? This right here is a doomsday list. I'm sorry to say it. But I won't lie to you."

"I hope this doesn't shock you when I tell you this," says Dani. "But there's quite a number of students in my school that have the same kind of list as I have."

"I wish it did shock me. I truly do. In an intelligent society where there's actual leadership, which we have too little of these days, the institutions of poison food capitalism would be outlawed."

"Well, I have a feeling," says Dani, "that if you said these things to most of the other girls in my school, who all seem brainwashed to like their fatness and want to see it normalized, they'd hate you for it. And if the government passed such a law as you suggest, there'd be an uprising."

Dani pushes her chair away from the table, saying, "Well, maybe the thing I need is what you needed—an *emergency plan*."

"Will you trust me?" asks Marian. "For it to work, you'll have to trust me."

"If you were born in 1951, that means you're sixty-seven. But I know fifty-year-olds that look older than you. I think I can trust you."

"You're too kind. But alright. It'll be an *Emergency Plan*, yours and mine. We'll work together. I'll help you. You won't understand everything. I myself don't even understand everything. The science of it boggles my mind. But sometimes all we need to make good dietary decisions is to understand *enough*. More will come later when you can begin to pick and choose different things.

"You can even eat a few things that aren't good for you, because your body is smart and it really can handle quite a bit of junk. But you must shift direction and get yourself to a better place of health first. Your body functions pretty well when it's healthy, and pretty poorly when it isn't. The problem with most people's diets is their bad habits. Going to a party where people are eating junk food and drinking pure sugar won't give you diabetes. But bringing that party to your home seven days a week will."

"I'm willing to follow your advice."

"There's also the topic of a choice you'll have later on," says Marian. "The question of whether or not to buy only organic foods. Since it would add to the cost, I think you should wait to make that decision. You're going to be eating a lot of vegetables in the next few months. Besides, to start out, we'll be eliminating a whole lot of poisons from your diet and from your body. So organic food can wait."

"Are you saying I'm full of poison?"

"Actually, you are. Remember this: poisons and toxic things are mostly stored in fat. You have a lot of fat. We're going to break up those fat molecules. When we do, a lot of water will be released into your system. You might have diarrhea. But when you break up those hydrogen molecules of fat, you'll be releasing all those toxins. You'll need to pee them out of you. So be prepared to drink a lot of just plain water."

"Alright then," says Dani. "How do we proceed?"

"I'm going to go around the store and put things in your cart. Most of the things on your list won't be in there. And this is going to be especially rough for your brother. You're going to have to give him encouragement to follow your plan. He won't like it. Your mother, too. She may be the greatest nurse in the world, but she doesn't seem to know very much about nutrition."

"Why can't I do this on my own and leave them out of it?"

"Because you don't want to leave them out of it. They need to eat healthy, too. And besides, there's something I haven't told you that you need to know. It's probably the most important two things about healthy eating that you need to know, and they're the two easiest things for you to remember and to do. First, before you go to the grocery store, be sure you've just eaten and are not hungry. Secondly, you must remember that dieting happens in the grocery store, not at home. Inside you is a hungry monster that will eat anything in sight. You can't go to the grocery store and buy junk and then come home and restrain that beast."

Dani hears the words, and the full weight of them falls on her. Her kitchen is about to turn into a war zone. "I don't have much of a chance, do I?"

"A thin thread of a chance. A little bitty one. It all depends on the power of your will to succeed and accomplish your goals. You said you want to be wealthy? I bet you want to find a nice boyfriend, too. But your doomsday list and catastrophic diet may be your biggest obstacles to reaching your goals. Well, there's no maybes about it. They *are*."

Dani scrunches up her nose. "Kinda like a snowball's chance, eh?"

"Kinda like maybe if you took and threw the snowball into a pot of boiling water. It all boils down to how badly you want to realize your dreams."

Sadly, Dani places both hands over her face. "Oh, what on earth am I gunna do? I can't come home without Crazy Louie's diet cola, corn chips, and salsa. And Mom's just gotta have her bagels and cream cheese—and I love those things, too."

23

At Fletcher's Market, Dani's journey begins anxiously as she follows Marian straight to the produce section. Although she isn't hungry now, there's a feeling a real wolf is lurking inside her, and all she has for courage is a very grown-up Little Red Riding Hood.

Trust her. You have to trust her.

In the way of actual produce, her doomsday list did have some: peas, carrots, corn, and broccoli, which Dani was planning to get from the frozen foods section. Not too bad, as Marian says, but not good enough.

"Why did you put your produce items at the bottom?" asks Marian.

Laughing, Dani says, "You mean peas, carrots, and broccoli? They're the just-in-case items."

"The what?"

"Just in case I have enough money to afford them."

"I guess that explains why you have your chips and crackers and ice cream at the top, your bread and bagels next, and pizza and frozen dinners after that."

"If I come home without the priorities, I'll be fired as a cook."

"Well, for the moment, can we just stick to the *Emergency Plan*? Your priorities are upside down, and we have to fix that." Marian makes a show of turning her list upside down to make her point.

"Alright, but I'll come knocking on your door if I get thrown out on the street."

In the produce section, Marian begins picking things off the shelves and loading the cart, naming them as she goes, starting with the kiosk where she takes up a whole bag of red grapefruit. "You are to eat half a pink grapefruit with every meal," she says. "This is for a host of reasons, so you must not leave it out. It provides important nutrients and vitamin C, and has relatively few calories as fruits go.

"For veggies, we want two heads of iceberg lettuce, a bunch of romaine, a bunch of Swiss chard, four large onions, a bunch of garlic cloves, Brussels sprouts, several cucumbers, six tomatoes, but some a bit green so they will ripen, several bunches of fresh broccoli, several green peppers and a few yellow and red ones for color. Let's not forget a few chili peppers, but only sparingly. Throw in a carrot or two. Oh, look, they have some fresh dandelion greens. These'll go well with your stir-fry or just cooked separately and served in a soup. Do you see anything that piques your interest?"

"What about zucchini and cucumbers?"

"Ah, a good idea!" Marian reaches up for a few long medium-sized zucchinis and several cucumbers.

"What are those up there?"

"That's ginger root. We'll take one. They're good for stir-fries, but more like a spice. You're going to be having a lot of stir-fries."

"What about asparagus?"

"Very good!" says Marian. "Asparagus will go well in a stir-fry or just on its own. See how your eyes take you to things? It could be your body telling you what it wants. You have to learn to follow what it tells you."

"It tells me it likes ice cream, a lot!"

"Don't start now. You've been good so far."

"Make it spinach, then."

"Spinach is good in small quantities. What else do you see? Your eyes can pick out things that are very good for you."

"You know I can't trust my eyes."

"You'll improve as you go."

"Haven't you heard of recidivism?" says Dani, laughing.

"Ha, ha . . . You're so funny, my dear child. Maybe you'll become a comedian. Now let's go to the meat department."

"What about those up there?"

Marian looks to see what it is. "Oh, sprouts! Very good eye! They'll go in your salads or stir-fries, but try them next time. You have enough for now. This'll last a few days and you'll be back to try different things. Let's check out the meats."

"Hey, what if I was a vegetarian? Or a vegan?"

"I'd tell you to read a few books on that topic. For our *Emergency Plan*, meat is definitely on it! You've got a growing body, and you need plenty of protein. This is no time to become a vegetarian. Veganism is a religion that draws on the currency of moral superiority. It opposes the natural order of things. So let's not discuss it any further. Anyway, many of the so-called vegetarians I know are fat. They think if it isn't meat, it must be alright. But that's not true. As you begin to read books about nutrition, you'll begin to read about lectins. You better study up on lectins. As they say in the Army, lectins are what separate the men from the boys."

"What are they?"

"They bind to certain sugars and cause bad things to happen. It's called agglutination and causes more or less the same problems as gluten does. Forget about it. It's not a topic you need to bother with right now. We're sticking with green vegetables and meat. For now, we've got to get that fat off you, and if you stick to our *Plan*, your fat will be disappearing like a snowball in boiling water."

At the meat counter, Marian picks out a large tray of 80% lean hamburger, noting for Dani the symbol showing the cows were *grass-fed*. She throws in a few steaks too as Dani calculates the prices in her head. She picks out two large trays of chicken breasts, noting the chickens are *free-range*. Then she goes over and takes some high-quality sausage, then two boxes of quality bacon, which Marian points out is *MSG- free*.

"What's MSG?" asks Dani.

"Monosodium glutamate. It's an additive flavor enhancer. Some people have reactions to it. I think it falls under the no-chemicals rule if you're in a grocery store. But if you go to a restaurant, as we all do, then you're going to get some anyway. I just try to avoid it whenever I can."

"Shall I always have to buy the most expensive items on the shelf?" asks Dani. "And isn't bacon like unbelievably fatty?"

"Dani, you get what you pay for. And you've been told lots of things that aren't true. There's bad fats and good fats. Did you know your body needs fat to burn fat?"

"That sounds like an oxymoron."

"You sure know some pretty fancy words."

"It means the statement contradicts itself," says Dani.

"Well, when it comes to fat, and that other little thing they call cholesterol, you'll learn there are a lot of contradictions, and also a lot of just plain bad science." Marian turns to Dani, looking at her straight on, and says, "Dani, there's one thing you've got to know right now. If you don't remember any other thing I've told you, please remember this: science has gone to pot!"

"I sorta got that already."

Marian turns and moves on.

"I'm going to have to freeze this meat," Dani says after her.

"Good point. Does your freezer work?"

"Yeah, but it's full."

"Full of what?"

"Mostly ice." Dani laughs. "Some ice cream. I've never seen the bottom of it. I think there may be things from the ice age in it. Certainly a lot of frozen veggies and a bunch of frozen orange juice."

"Good. You'll be throwing the ice cream away. Then you'll be digging the veggies out and using them in your stir-fries, which I'm going to show you how to cook. Remind me to get some freezer paper. And by the way, you're going to stop drinking frozen juices or any kind of juices. No fruit juices for you!"

"None? Never? And never any ice cream?"

"No. In dieting, nothing is never. Just for now. This is an *emergency*, remember? The ice cream won't be any good in six months. So it's best to throw it away. But you'll never eat much of it ever again. Now, do you have a wok?"

"No. But what am I going to do about fruit? Vitamin C. Everybody makes all this fuss about eating five fruits a day."

"Grapefruit will help with that. But you can add more fruits after your *emergency* has passed. And thank you for reminding me to mention vitamins. It's an important topic. We'll have to have a talk about that. But we'll save it for another time. As for vitamin C, you'll pick up quite a bit of that in your emergency diet. But do remind me, when you've lost your weight and things begin to settle down, we need to have a talk about serious exercise and vitamins, along with a good balanced diet. There are a few vitamins you'll need to take every day to boost your immune system. A few important ones are vitamins D and K, and there's zinc, in winter especially. But vitamins are tricky and you need to know more about them. So, where was I?"

"You asked about a wok?"

"Ah, yes. So you'll need one."

They come to the dairy section and Marian puts a pound of actual butter in her cart. "Breakfast is the most important meal and you must eat specific things for your breakfast every day in order to start your metabolism out right. For your breakfasts—for the duration of this plan—you'll be eating two slices of bacon, two eggs fried in the bacon fat, and half a grapefruit peeled and cut into pieces. You'll eat no toast, no bagels, no cream cheese. For the rest of the day, eat only the green vegetables and meat, but only small amounts of meat. And remember, some things they call vegetables are not even vegetables. No peas, no lima beans, no garbanzo beans, no corn. Absolutely no corn in any form! Do you hear me?"

Marian turns to her.

Dani forces the grin off her face.

"Listen, you little corn eater, this is it and it's simple: for breakfast it's two eggs, two strips of bacon. For lunch and dinner you'll eat only green vegetables and meat—salads, stir-fry, any way you want to eat them. Eat a good full bowl of salad or a good dish of stir-fry. Stick to this same daily diet for the duration of the diet. Some people suggest breaking it up into two-week segments and taking three or four days off. But I never took days off. In fact, I'm pretty much still on the diet now, except for a bit of bread now and then and a bit of fruit and once in a while a small bit of pie or peach cobbler. I like this diet. And I think you'll like it, too. And with each meal you'll eat a half a grapefruit on the side or a quarter of one if they're large. And you can't leave anything out."

"Why grapefruit, though? Why not an orange or banana?" asks Dani.

"I prefer grapefruit mostly because it's a fruit that's low in calories and is very good for you if you're not taking certain meds. Are you taking any meds?"

"No."

"Good. So don't worry about it. If you were taking meds like statins, blood thinners or estrogen, then I'd say ask your doctor if you should eat grapefruit. But I think grapefruit increases the HDL cholesterol, so I like eating it, and it has vitamin C. Some people think it helps burn fat, but I know from the times I haven't had grapefruit, I still lose the weight. But it doesn't interfere with weight loss and it provides a bit of color and ambiance to every meal, like a little side-dish treat. So I should have asked if you're taking any meds. Like heart medications. A person on meds probably already has a list of things they shouldn't be eating with their meds."

"Well, I'm not on any meds."

"Well, then I think grapefruit makes a nice threesome for your breakfast and it will provide you with vitamin C if it does nothing else.

"You know, I eat lunch provided by the school," says Dani.

"Oh, my god, no!"

Dani laughs out loud. "You know, you should be the comedian."

"Sorry, school lunches are not funny and they're not on the *plan*. You eat a big salad for lunch every day. Bring it in a big tub."

"It's a lot of work to make a salad, you know."

"No, it isn't. You make the salad in bulk, washing your lettuce and preparing all the ingredients at one time. You take an entire head of lettuce and make a big tub of chopped lettuce. Use another big tub for the other ingredients. You prepare the things in advance and in bulk. Don't mix them because lettuce doesn't last as long as some of the other things and you'll want to keep your lettuce bin fresh. Do you have any large plastic bins with sealable covers?"

"No."

"So we'll get two of them. Do you have a salad spinner?"

"No. I've never even heard of a salad spinner."

"We'll get the things you need. It's all part of the *Plan*."

At the olive oil section, Marian carefully selects a large metal can and shows Dani the label, which says *extra virgin, cold pressed*. When Dani sees the price, blood rushes from her face and she nearly faints.

"Don't worry, it lasts a long time," says Marian. "Oh, here's another thing I forgot to mention." Marian picks up a large bottle of coconut oil. "You will use this for your cooking oil. No vegetable oils! Do you hear me?"

"Why not?"

"It goes along with the no margarine thing. Never mind. Too much information will split your skull. Just don't use vegetable oils! Use coconut oil for cooking and olive oil and vinegar for making salad dressing."

They go to the coffee section, and Marian places a pound of coffee into the cart. "Finally, something from my actual list!" says Dani. "But it's really for my mother. She says I shouldn't drink coffee, but I do like it."

"Coffee's very good for dieting. It tends to reduce hunger pangs. Besides, I might want some when I come to visit."

"I want you to visit. I want you to be there when we have our first actual meal at the dining table, even if it's only you and me."

"Your mom will love the new diet. You'll see. And Louis—he's a growing boy. I bet he's tired of eating junk. I'm sure he'll love your stir-fries. It might be a challenge to get him into salads, though. But as soon as he sees you trimming up, he'll decide to join you. You watch, when people see others looking healthier, they'll want to be healthier, too."

"Would you stay for lunch today?" asks Dani. "Maybe show me how to make a good salad? And tomorrow, would you come back and show me how to make a stir-fry? Then my mother will be home to join us. I think she'd really like to meet you."

"I'd love to."

"Both?"

"Sure. Lunch today and dinner tomorrow," says Marian. "We'll make us a stir-fry like none other."

"I can't wait."

Dani takes a deep breath, feeling energized over having a brand new friend.

They move on to the salad dressings. "What kind do you like?"

"Blue Cheese."

"You know what?" Marian puts her finger on her chin and for a moment feigns deep thought. "I'll tell you what. Since you're an Italian girl, I think you prefer Italian dressing. Vinegar and oil. Isn't that so?"

Dani starts to laugh again. "Oh, alright. I really love vinegar and oil."

All the dressings are buy-one-get-one-at-half-price, and Marian takes two bottles of the balsamic vinegar and two of extra spicy Italian, but turns to the ingredients label. "See here, be sure to check to see they use olive oil and not vegetable oil. Don't ask me why. We don't have time to get into it and you can do your own reading on this. But for me, I prefer to make my own salad dressing, but you've got enough to think about. But we can get some apple cider vinegar so you can try your hand at making your own dressing—save the store-bought dressing for when you don't have time or want a little variety. But remember, make sure they're using olive oil. Do you hear me? Olive. Oil. Good-quality store-bought salad dressing is going to cost more, just like everything else."

"How do you make your own?"

"When you use up your store-bought dressings, save the glass bottles and try to buy everything in glass containers, OK? Just remember that. Then you'll have a few bottles with small lids."

"Why not plastic?"

"Just take my word. We want to avoid plastics. Glass is better. You can look it up for yourself. Now, where were we?"

"You were saying about the salad bottles."

"Yes, save a few with the lids for mixing your salad dressing. You mix half olive oil and half apple cider vinegar, throw in some spices you like, and shake it real well. You can be very creative with spices. You can even spice it up with a few of those hot peppers minced up. You put it all together and let it stand overnight. Don't refrigerate it. Do you hear me? No refrigeration! Shake it well, and you've got yourself a nice salad dressing."

They pick up a roll of freezer paper, then go over to where the pots and pans are and see two kinds of woks.

"This one's no-stick," says Dani, picking it up.

"And this one's steel," says Marian. "The old-fashioned kind."

"But this one's easier to wash," counters Dani.

"And this one isn't coated with chemicals." Marian makes a cute face.

"Yours is more expensive," says Dani.

"Exactly!" says Marian, placing the heavy steel one in the cart.

Marian also takes up a handsome bamboo cutting board along with a new vegetable peeler. They then turn their attention to finding a salad spinner. But Marian notices the large stainless steel colander. "Do you have a good colander?"

"No. I just pour off the water from the pan."

"Alright. I think it's a good idea to keep away from plastics as much as possible, and you don't have a lot of money to play with, so let's go with the stainless colander. It's more efficient and you need one for other things."

"Like pasta," says Dani grinning.

"Some day pasta, yes. When you weigh— Hey, what's your goal?"

"One fifteen, one-twenty."

"When you reach your goal, I'll treat you to a spaghetti dinner. Chicken parmesan and a small sip of wine. But first, the *Plan!*"

24

There comes a time when the grocery cart seems to be getting full. Yet when Dani takes her shopping list in hand, she sees hardly anything that's on the list is in the cart.

"Hmm."

She follows Marian to the spices, where her advisor picks out all the common ones such as oregano, garlic, turmeric, black pepper, parsley, and Italian seasoning. Dani sees the ground onion and throws that in for good measure.

"These are mostly for your stir-fry and salad dressing," says Marian. "There are some good recipes for salad dressing, so you can experiment when you have time."

Dani keeps looking at her list. "What about cinnamon? What about nutmeg and allspice? What about raisins, oranges, and apples? What about blueberries? Oh my god! What about pie crusts? Couldn't I at least make pancakes and muffins for Mom and Louie, and an apple pie? You're taking all the fun out of my being a cook!"

Marian steps over and takes the list from her hand and proceeds to fold it up into a little pocket-size thing, which she stuffs into Dani's fat sweatpants pocket. "You're done with your list. Tuck it into your journal page. Someday you'll open it and read it and have a good laugh."

"I don't keep a journal."

"Dani, if you prepare pies and pancakes for your family, you'll be eating those things, too. If you deviate one little bit from the plan, you'll not lose weight and all our time will have been wasted. Do you hear me? You've got to stick to the *Plan!* Now say it for me. You've got to…what?"

"Stick to the *Plan!*"

"Marian points her finger at her and looks her in the eye. "And don't forget it. If you wanna be successful in anything, you gotta have a *Plan* and you gotta *stick to your Plan!*"

Dani stands there feeling the weight of this—how completely transformed will be the diet of her entire family.

"Look, if you want me to, I'll speak to your mom."

"No. That's not necessary. I'll talk to her. I want her to think this is coming from me, not you."

"Good. I want it to come from you also. As for those other spices, they're not required for the *Plan*. They're for cooking fancy dishes and desserts, foods heavy in calories and sugars. It looks like you were planning quite a variety of fancy dishes with some fancy recipes."

"Yeah. Just to add a bit of va-ri-e-tee."

"Va-ri-e-tee is fine for later and for rare occasions. Your weight loss goal comes first. How much weight are we losing?"

"It's gotta be like . . . a lot."

"How much? You've set your goal. How much do you need to lose?"

Dani scrunches up her nose. "I'm pushing one-ninety most of the time, give or take a grace day."

"Well, don't lose heart. You'll get there. But for now, we need to get you started. All you need to do is…what?"

Lamentingly: "Stick to the *Plan!*"

"If you want to achieve your goals," adds Marian, "you better do as I say!"

"So all I'm going to eat is eggs and bacon and stir-fry and salad? Then what?"

"When you reach your goal, you can eat more regular meals. If you want to take a break for a few days, you can eat a few balanced meals. But no junk food or cola. Maybe you'd like to have some white rice with your stir-fry, or throw in some pineapple. Yeah, that's an idea. Let's go get a pineapple for your stir-fries…for when you take a break from your plan."

"So, when I go on a break from my diet, which is mostly stir-fry, I get to throw in a little pineapple?"

"Yeah, sure…run and get a fresh one. You can set it in the window. Pineapples love the sun and are all full of energy, just like you'll be when you lose all that weight. Something tells me you're a girl who loves the sun, too."

Dani goes and gets the pineapple. What sort of trick is Marian trying to play on her…having always to see such a sweet and delicious fruit, but rarely able to taste it. "This will be like torturing me," she says bringing it back and placing it in the cart.

"It'll give you some discipline," says Marian. "Help teach you abstinence, which you're going to need a lot of when you get thin, cause boys are bound to notice."

"You think?" Dani grins.

"Do I think?!"

Dani giggles.

"I'm afraid to tell you. Your troubles are only just beginning, my little sweet tooth."

"Is that a promise?"

"You do know, don't you, I may be creating a monster here."

"Nah. I'm just a harmless little sweet tooth."

"We'll just see how harmless you are after you lose seventy pounds and boys start to follow you around. And you better stay away from that pineapple…no matter how much you crave it. Think of it as a temptation."

"You mean I should think of it as a boy."

"I didn't say that." Marian grins coyly.

"What other treats may I have on a break…that I can look forward to?"

"Maybe for breakfast you could fix up a cheese omelet."

"What about bagels, and cream cheese? And pancakes? Can I eat a pizza?"

"How badly do you really want this, Dani?"

"I guess pretty bad. Since you mentioned it, I guess I'm curious about how *harmlessly* bad I can really be."

"You guess you're curious, eh? Well, I should tell you, harmless girls can cause a lot of trouble. Take my word. I've raised a few boys."

"Real bad, eh? Very, very, very bad?"

"Let's put it this way. If you can stay away from that pineapple long enough, you're going to find out. I just hope you don't have to learn about it the hard way."

"Sounds ominous. But don't worry. I'm on this. I'm on it and I won't disappoint you. Once I start losing weight, I'll just go ahead and let that pineapple rot. There'll be no breaks for me!"

"Oh, I almost forgot," says Marian. "Follow me."

Marian takes her to the soup shelves, and they find the organic bone broths. She takes up one for beef and one for chicken. "Now you can make stew if you like. Vegetables, meat, and, oh, I forgot, go and fetch me a head of cabbage."

"Hey," says Dani, turning back. "What about those potatoes?"

"Sorry. No. Not even on your break. That's the kind that require peeling. So don't buy them. But when you've lost all the weight you want to lose, maybe *someday* you can eat real potatoes…now and then—for Thanksgiving, Christmas, and Easter."

Dani is tempted to pick up a few things for Crazy Louie and her mom, but has heard about enough of Marian's drill sergeant voice for one day. She passes the snack and beverage aisles and doesn't even turn to look at the ice cream freezers. She returns with the cabbage and places it in the cart.

"How much have you spent?" asks Marian.

"I estimate about seventy-five dollars, but we'll say it's a hundred."

"Well, there's room for more. Why don't we go back and pick up a few more off your list?"

"No. I've decided not to. It's gunna be all or nothing. If they want their junk, they can go get it themselves!"

"That's my girl."

"Oh, and I have one more thing to get." Dani runs off into the store, returning with a box of four tall dining candles.

25

It's amazing how little extra space is necessary to store $130 worth of food, except, of course, for the refrigerator itself.

Marian has come in with her from the store, and together they find room for all the things. Marian cuts the freezer paper into sheets for wrapping the meat, dividing it into smaller meal portions, making it easier to thaw just enough for one meal. Dani notices how small the meal portions are and how little space the meat requires in the freezer once it's wrapped. They use a felt marker to label it.

"So the *plan* is, like, almost vegetarian, eh?" she complains.

"The problem with meat isn't that people eat it; it's that people eat way too much of it."

Marian shows her how to open the container of olive oil, then takes out the stainless colander, vegetable peeler, new cutting board, and wok and washes them, scrubbing to get off any shipping oils from the wok. Since the refrigerator is packed full of unmentionable things, they go through it and take everything out of it and toss most of it in the garbage can. There is a pile of plastic containers on the counter. Dani washes them and Marian helps her wash out the refrigerator drawers and shelves and the area below the drawers, which has layers of goop dried on from years of spilling. They wash the refrigerator top to bottom and even roll it forward and clean the floor under it. They remove all the old paper bags that are wedged in beside it and many that have fallen behind it. For all its abuses inside and out, it's amazing the poor refrigerator works at all.

"Your refrigerator has to breathe," says Marian. "If you block the airflow, it won't work properly. You could have a fire."

"That would be one way to get a clean house," says Dani.

Marian wasn't much for joking about fires and showed no sign of laughing. "Obviously, you haven't any experience with fires."

Marian is fastidious in her cleaning. Grandma Anita is like that too—every detail a big deal, endless cleaning and fussing. Dani's never liked cleaning anything. But somehow, working with Marian and seeing how much enthusiasm she puts into it, Dani begins to see how taking care of one's body might dovetail with taking care of the place you store your food—it's all part of a whole and complete picture. Grandma Anita used to insist she make her bed every morning; she insisted on it even if Dani and Cindy slept in the cabin. She scolded them if they didn't. She scolded them if they didn't bathe in Prism Lake with the all-natural soaps she left there for bathing at the end of every day. She scolded them if they did not hang up their towels and put away their things neatly. She would not let them throw down their shoes, but made them set their shoes neatly one beside the other. *Suppose you have to leave in a hurry. Maybe there's a fire in the night. Are you going to stop and look all over for your shoes?*

If they cuddled under a blanket while watching television in the evening, before going to bed Grandma Anita made them fold the blanket neatly and place the pillows in their proper places. She told them over and again *if the spaces around you are not in good order then the spaces within you will not be in good order also.*

Watching Marian there, Dani is beginning to understand it.

"Marian, I want to thank you for all your time helping me. You've gone way beyond just giving me a bit of advice. But I have a question still. Could I ask how you stay so darned happy?"

"You've been so patient all day, Dani. I'm quite surprised. For your age, you've taken in an awful lot of information in a short time. You probably won't remember it all. But do try to remember this: everything we've done today—our walks together and our talk over breakfast, our shopping, our cleaning your refrigerator and organizing your shelves—it all goes together. From the moment you get out of bed in the morning until you put your head down on your pillow at night, all of your spaces affect your mood. The key is to ask yourself what brings *you* joy, what lifts *you* up in your spirits? Take and break down your hours and minutes, even your seconds. Try to remember the little things that perked up your spirits. Think about what lifts your self-esteem. Ask yourself how you might have more of those moments. Ask what you want from life. Focus on the long term. What makes you proud? I never quite understood why God put pride on the list of capital sins. I wish more people were proud. Perhaps God thinks of pride as feeling superior to others, putting ourselves on a pedestal of vainglory. But I see pride more as a feeling of having done something well for which you feel a quiet sense of accomplishment. I think God wants us to do good work and to be focused on the quality of our work—doing something for the sake of having done it well, not merely for money. If all we work for is money, I'm afraid the quality of our work will suffer. But if we work to always lift ourselves up into joy, well, now you can see why a person might feel joy while getting their hands dirty at a cleaning project or doing something as mundane as making their bed in the morning."

"Now that you mention it," says Dani, "making my bed in the morning is one of the things that lifts my spirits and makes me feel better about myself." She laughs. "And getting that refrigerator clean has made me happy, too. Thank you."

"The thing that will always lift you up in your spirits is being a model for others, so they can be lifted up, too."

In this way, Marian and Dani make room for all the veggies and the big plastic salad bins that take up half a shelf. Marian helps her wash whatever dishes are sitting around; then she clears off the counters. They clean off the kitchen table, too, throwing away a lot of things.

When all this is finished, Marian turns her attention to the dining room table, which is cluttered with all sorts of things like school books, several boxes containing board games, coats hanging on the backs of chairs, newspapers and magazines piled in stacks, many looking like they've never been read. Of course, there's a big pile of mail. The dining table hasn't been used for dining because mostly Dani and Louie have most all their meals in their bedrooms and her mother eats in the kitchen. A meal with all of them together, as Dani sees it, only serves to remind them of the family catastrophe.

When the clutter is put away, Dani takes a washcloth and cleans off many months' worth of dust and grime. Suddenly the old wooden table looks shiny and suitable for a family meal. Marian washes the chairs, then takes it one step further, asking Dani if there are any placemats. To Dani's surprise, she finds these in the china cabinet drawer, nice-looking mats with spring flowers on them. She places four of them around the table. She then goes to her pantry where she put the new candles. Taking one from the box and finding an old candle holder in the china cabinet, she places the candle in the middle of the table. Dani and Marian stand there surveying the table for a moment. Of course, the room itself is jammed full of things that also need putting away. But it's a nice sight just the same, the table all cleared off and the varnish gleaming in the sunlight. It's a good beginning.

"Now let's make a lunch!" says Marian, putting her hands together. "What shall we fix?"

"Oh, let's see." Dani puzzles a moment, placing her fingers to her chin, then says, "I know. Why don't we have a salad with a few strips of chicken?"

"With Italian dressing?" suggests Marian.

"Hey, that's a great idea! And, you know what? Let's throw in a half grapefruit on the side!"

26

*D*ani knocks on the bedroom door and shouts, "Louie!"

"What?!"

Can you open the door, please?"

Louis opens the door and stands there facing her, obviously unhappy that she's interrupted his video game.

"You want to have lunch with Aunt Marian and me? We're having grilled chicken breast on a big salad, with grapefruit on the side."

"She's not our aunt, you know."

"How do you know? She could be. Lots of Italians from Sicily are related. It's an island, you know."

He scoffs.

"Come on. You'll love our new diet. We're going to get healthy. We're going to stop eating like pigs. We're going to lose weight. All of us."

The question poses so contrary an idea he can't seem to wrap his brain around it. He merely stares at her like a zombie, finally asking, "What are you *talking* about?"

"You must have missed the memo. I slid it under your door this morning."

Louis looks on the floor and Dani laughs out loud.

"Eff-you a memo!"

"Well, I'll give it to you now. We have a new diet. We're getting off junk food. We're going to lose weight. We're going to shape up this ship. We're taking off the fat. Peeling down. And Mom, too. All of us. Every one of us. And we're starting today. Right now." She draws out her phone and taps the face of it and points to the time. "This minute now."

"A diet!" he scoffs and laughs. "You've been on so many diets I can't even count em all."

He starts pushing the door shut on her, but she steps in with her foot blocking it. "I'm losing seventy pounds. You're losing— hmmm, I think maybe fifty would do it for you. At least. Maybe more."

Louie studies her a moment longer, seemingly dazed or maybe just waiting for her to laugh at her own joke.

"I'm going to be fixing healthy meals and losing this stupid weight." She pats her bulging tummy. "You can join me or you can just keep on getting fatter."

"Healthy meals…I've heard *that* before, like an old black and white rerun! It usually means I have to starve to death."

"Alright then. If you wanna keep buying your junk food, then be my guest, but I'm not bringing it into the house and I'm not paying for it. But I will certainly make sure you have a nice funeral. With lots of flowers. What would you like on your headstone? Oh, I have an idea:

HERE LIES CRAZY LOUIE
WHO DIED VERY YOUNG.
AND HERE'S THE SAD SONG THAT WE SUNG.
HE BENT HIS BIKE PEDDLES,
AND HIS SKATEBOARD SAGGED.
HE BROKE HIS FAT ARMS
AND ALMOST HIS FAT HEAD.
YET NOTHING STOPPED HIM
BUT HIS CORN CHIPS AND SALSA,
WHICH HE ATE IN HIS BED.

"You do know you're a jerk, right?" he says, trying to push the door shut, but her foot doesn't budge.

"No. What I am is fat! And ugly! And so are you!"

He stands there considering the vast algorithm of his options.

"You won't starve," she says. "But it won't be easy either."

"So what sort of food is it?"

"Never mind. You'll see. You'll like it."

Louie gives her a puckered scowl like somebody just took away his comic books.

"Are we just gunna keep getting fatter and fatter, Louie, till we waddle like ugly ducks quack quack?"

His room is a mess, strewn with dirty clothes. His bed is unmade. He has posters of skiers and skateboarders and snowboarders. One poster of some skimpy swimsuit model. "You think *you're* gunna get a girl like that?" she asks, eyeing the lovely girl. She then points to another poster. "Does *he* look fat to you?"

Louie turns and looks at the poster of Shaun White on a snowboard.

"It will be rude if you don't join us," she says. "And I think Marion wants to talk to you about a job."

"What kind of job?"

"Different things. Her son's looking for some help with stuff. They have apartment houses. All kinds of stuff. For the whole summer. Money in your pocket so you can buy your own poison to eat in your bed."

"Alright," he says. "But you're still a jerk."

"Put on something nicer. And comb your hair. You know what? A shower wouldn't hurt. It'll be ready in half an hour."

27

Marian sets out the new bamboo cutting board on the table, then takes out one whole chicken breast, which is not yet frozen, removing this from its wrapping paper. She cuts the breast into long and very thin strips. Then, after putting in a tablespoon of coconut oil, she sets the gas flame on medium/low so as not to overheat the oil, and lets the pan get hot, then places the strips into the sizzling oil and adds some garlic, chopped onion, and pepper. It's a neat process and Dani watches.

"You're doing what Mrs. Kanbury taught us to do in Home Ec class."

"What's that?"

"How to make a little meat go a long way by slicing it thin."

Marian smiles. "That's it. Works every time. But there's another little trick I bet she didn't teach you. That's to make up more than one meal a time. This'll be enough for your lunch tomorrow, too."

"But if you're coming over for dinner, I'll just skip lunch."

"That's another thing," says Marian. "You can't skip meals. No skipping. You must eat breakfast, lunch, and dinner. If you skip, you'll be so hungry by dinnertime you'll be too tempted to overeat or snack on something."

While the chicken is cooking, Marian and Dani turn their attention to making the salad by first washing the cutting board thoroughly with soap and hot water to wash off all residue from the raw chicken. They then take and chop the head of lettuce in half, chopping one half into bite-size pieces, then rinsing and shaking it in the colander. They chop up the carrots and cucumbers into diagonal slices. They add a tomato, cube-chopped. Marian has Dani slice a large dill pickle along with some broccoli crowns. She chops a red and a green pepper in bite-size pieces, adding on top some thinly sliced red onions and chili peppers chopped in round slices with radishes thrown on top.

In this way, Dani and Marian proceed to make Dani's first actual meal in her first very own kitchen. When all is ready, Marian takes one of the grapefruits from the dining table fruit basket, a basket which Dani found in a drawer of the china cabinet beside the placemats. She proceeds to show Dani how to peel it, using the new peeling tool they used on the carrots, zucchini, and cucumbers. Once peeled, Marian slices the grapefruit in thirds, chops these sections into small bite-size pieces, and puts them into three small bowls that she finds in the china cabinet, which happens to be full of a fine old set of china that hasn't been used in so long she has to rinse off the dust.

"Louie!" calls Dani up the stairs.

He comes out of his room dressed in jeans and a fairly acceptable button-up school shirt with its tails tucked in. Amazing. His hair is still wet from his shower but combed back neatly. More amazing. Louie has those sharp eyes like Dani's. He's a handsome boy the girls will go for when he loses his fifty pounds. Dani is surprised and very pleased, and she follows him into the dining room, and they sit at the table, but first, Dani goes and gets the igniter, using this to light the candle.

"Would you like to say grace, Aunt Marian?"

They bow their heads, and Marian proceeds with a short blessing:

> "Oh, Lord, thank you
> for this meal and our fellowship.
> We pray you'll guide us so we may
> put its use to thy use. Amen."

Marian crosses herself, and Dani quickly follows her lead, as does Louie, as there is a certain moment of quiet, and the illumination of the candle seems aglow with something holy. It isn't quite the same as when she goes to church and takes communion, the high mass being held in the actual House of the Lord, but Dani can feel something spiritual is definitely here nonetheless, like a connection to the past and also to the future, a feeling of being part of what's gone before as well as the future to come. She thinks of her father, who can't work, and her mother the nurse, and of the little girl Marian, picking beans with her mom while her dad fixed cars. She thinks of Marian's first husband, who died in Vietnam, and of her second husband Mack who built and remodeled houses.

She also thinks of Cindy Rand.

Fact is, all through this process, from the day she met Marian, she's been thinking of Cindy and feeling very close to her, and missing her, such ideas she put in her head that she might one day shed her fat costume and be beautiful. She's going to stick to this diet come what may. And soon as she has a chance, she's going to thank Cindy and tell her she loves her also.

But these thoughts seem to get smothered in conflicting doubts—the sins of vanity and pride and her growing desire to find a boy to love like Cindy has.

~

THE END OF BOOK ONE

ACKNOWLEDGMENT

Special Note of Thanks

No part of our story was written by artificial intelligence, nor was any part of the creative writing assisted by AI, including storyline and plot. We use Apple Intelligence to assist with proofreading.

However, we wish to thank Grok, created by xAI, for its help in advising on the topic of publishing the work. Having Grok as a publishing advisor has been invaluable. Thank you, xAI for creating Grok.

— H.R. Novelton

COMING SOON

DANI BOOK 2 : *The Three-Sided Coins Or The Good Zone Plan*

Dani's a girl who in Book One faced monumental body image issues. But taking the advice from her new friend, and with steely determination, she now faces a whole new set of problems she never bargained for—how to protect herself from herself.

The beauty coin seems to have three sides. It seems beauty comes in a package: one side is what you get when you quit with your unhealthy habits, lose seventy pounds, and peel off the mask that hides a girl of the Northeast Tribes; the second part is love and sex, which comes drifting in and tries to swallow you up; and the third part is your dreams and how you and your brand-new beautiful self are a threat to them.

DANI BOOK 3 : *Stand for Something or The Blood Never Forgets*

The cliché becomes real when one is tested. First, it's Dani's brother Crazy Louie when he's attacked by a gang in the park; then it's Dani herself. Life happens unexpectedly. It's when we find out how fragile the threads that ground us are, how medicine works when we really need it to open portals to let out pain and to let in joy.

DANI BOOK 4 : *What About Love? or Medicine Of The Mountain*

When hope seems nigh, Dani is now to face her biggest sorrow. In Book Four, we turn our attention to a mountain that harmonizes and heals. The story folds together, events seem to have purposes, and the sky opens to a future that wants to sing.

∽

Other Books by H.R. Novelton, LLC (Available)

A MESSAGE TO TIGER LILY : *How We Found Our Way Home*

Most suitable as a book to be read aloud to children. The story takes us on a high-road adventure as a lonely chipmunk, who learns his name is Genius (mistakenly), meets a host of new friends and traveling companions who are also lost and alone and ready for someone with courage to lead them to a new and better life. Topics of interest include: the importance of keeping promises; the value of friendship and the duty to uplift those you love even if that means you must give up a few of your egotistical advantages; the value of teamwork; and how seeing yourself in others can make you a true genius.